THE SWEET SHOP DIARIES

Walter Jones

THE COMEDIC MUSINGS OF A SWEET ENTREPRENEUR

VOLUME 1

First published in Great Britain in 2013 by Mastersafe Limited

40, Spierbridge Road, Storrington, West Sussex, RH20 4PG

The moral right of David Burns to be identified

as the author of this work has been asserted.

Copyright © David Burns 2013

Cover designer Andy Ashdown Designs

Illustrations by David Burns

Illustrations © David Burns 2013

All rights reserved.
No part of this publication may be reproduced, stored in a
retrieval system or transmitted in any form or by any means
electronic, mechanical, photocopying, recording or
otherwise, without the prior written permission of the author.

ISBN: 978-0-9927539-0-0

Printed and bound in England.

Dedication

To Sarah.

I remember the day I walked with you down the aisle –

you were working at Sainsbury's.

And

To Mum and Dad.

Dad, would you stop running around so much

and let Mum catch up with you!

Mum, have you tried putting something in his coffee?

Contents

Acknowledgements	vi
Foreword by Louise	vii
Introduction – Opening Up	1
Are You Kidding?	5
The Sweet Old Orange Lady	13
French Jedi Warriors	21
Police, Camera, No Action!	33
Dish It With Denise	41
Fit And Healthy	51
Mr Cool	57
The Rubbish Magician	63
Do It Yourself	77
Unusual Italian Lollies	87
The Safest Form Of Transport	93
The Chase	99
The Tattooed Man	105
Walter In Hospital	111
She Who Must Be Obeyed	123
Nibble, Nibble, Nibble	131
Looking Back	141
Say It With Sweets	153
Closing Up	161
And Finally	167

Acknowledgements

What is this? Some kind of Oscar speech? Well, here goes.

I'd firstly like to thank all my longsuffering customers. Their quirky behaviour and unusual questions have been an inspiration. I no longer feel the odd one out.

Roy Stannard (www.zerofiftyone.com) has been great with his encouragement and magic when it comes to advertising. What a genius.

Andy Ashdown dreams and comes up trumps with the greatest book cover designs. I'm grateful for his patience with all the alterations I wanted. A truly brilliant job. My wife also says he's a very nice man.

To the Weald School, especially Jane Nailen, who helped me with the difficult task of choosing a cover design. Her idea to ask staff, younger students and sixth-formers for their comments and feedback on the initial designs was more than I could have asked. Thank you so much, staff and students!

To Andrew who reminded me how rude I was. This only helped to confirm that I was on the right track…

Lastly, thank you Louise for telling me to keep writing.

Foreword by Louise

Walter asked me to write the 'Foreword' because he said that it sounded like the best word to describe my interactions with men.

Forward? Me? Better *forward* than *backward*, Walter. I'll push you forward, forward off a cliff with the prod of one of your very own liquorice sticks! Don't think I will be laying marshmallows out for your landing either, you old…

So anyway, you see, it all started when I was working in a bar. "Nice Eyebrows." a man said. I looked scornfully at him as he continued, "I'm working my way down." Well!

Walter says I'm forward but this was too much. I couldn't work there any longer and I had to find myself a new job and quickly. Somewhere where I would get the respect I deserved as a young lady.

It was the middle of summer but a rather miserable day, as I recall. I was walking through the town despairing of my current work situation when I noticed the old sweet shop. This could be the trick to cheer me up I thought!

I strolled in and there he was, a funny looking man, telling inappropriate jokes about large ladies and flirting with an elderly blind woman.

His name was Walter Jones and he was looking for staff.

Introduction - Opening Up

"Just a minute! Have you paid for that chocolate bar?" I exclaimed.

"But I'll be hungry later." came the reply.

"That's no excuse to help yourself to chocolate bars without paying!" I retorted.

"But Daddy, it was in the fridge and Mummy said I could have one in my packed lunch."

Old habits die hard and I sometimes forget to adjust when I'm not at work.

My little shop is a real old fashioned sweet shop. It has all the original features and two bay windows where I display a myriad of sugary treats. And it's very popular. The old ladies queue for ages to get in. Some have been known to arrive at least five minutes before I open up. No sooner is the key turned in the lock that they 'zimmer' their way in towards the jars of liquorice, barley sugars and sherbet lemons.

I've noticed a great many new sweet shops around but my shop is over a hundred years old. Great Granddad Jones inherited it from his father and I inherited it one day from mine. It was a bit of a surprise.

"I'm off now, Son. You mind the shop for me while I embark on a worldwide cruise." my father said. It took him ten years – he neglected to tell me that Mother was rowing him.

Still, I've been here for some time now and I'm glad you've found me and popped in at last. Just where have you been? Come on, let me show you around my shop.

On the left there's our speciality rack of lollies, dozens of different ones and a really unusual one you'll read about later. On the right there are boxes of Belgian chocolates, bags of Italian nougat and tins of fruity boiled treats.

Further down on your left you'll find traditional sticks of liquorice and original chew bars and over on the right a magnificent unrivalled rack of jelly beans, fudge and assorted gift boxes.

Head towards the counter and you'll discover bars of artisan chocolate, crates of Turkish delight and four hundred jars of the most wonderful original sweets you can still remember from when you were just a tot.

Welcome to my world! I'll leave you to explore…

Walter

Livingstone also discovered the source of the Sherbet Falls.

Are You Kidding?

MIDGET GEM

WALTER: What can I get you, Frank?

FRANK: Jelly babies please!

WALTER: Do you want the large quiet ones dusted in talcum powder or the mini ones that wake up crying?

In summertime the shop is swarming with kids. It seems to me that the school holidays and our proximity to the beach creates the ideal combination to attract these 'pre-people'. Don't get me wrong - some kids are great. I love them. Especially the ones that are restrained. Others are just wild. They're all over the place and, like a pack of marauding hyenas, they attack my shelves in fits of laughter.

Thinking about children and wild animals, have you ever been to the zoo? I remember going there as a child. Never with my parents because we were just too poor. My father would pretend the pet shop was the local zoo, or he'd take me to the supermarket if I wanted to see farm animals.

DAD: Look, Son, there's a chicken!

WALTER: But it's got no head or feathers?

DAD: Never mind about that, Son. Beneath that plastic packaging it's still a real, genuine chicken. Look at the way it's curled up neatly, with its legs tied together.

WALTER: Can't we see a wild one?

DAD: Wild one? They can be dangerous. Many children have been known to be attacked by rabid chickens. No, it's much safer here in captivity.

WALTER: But this is a supermarket?

DAD: It's captivity to me when your mother takes me shopping. Come on, I want to show you some pigs camouflaged as sausages.

My father wasn't cruel - just very much untrained in the domesticated world of children. You have to remember that in those days the culture was so different. For example, in keeping with his early 'Teddy Boy' image, my father's approach to keeping babies and toddlers happy was to ply them with sweet cigarettes. He was never mean, though. You see, despite my father's lack of sensitivity to a seven year old boy, he did manage to scrape together enough coins to pay for school excursions.

The annual school trip to London Zoo holds great memories, not least because the most popular kid in the class was so travel sick that he'd spend most of the journey throwing up into a bag. Of course, no one wanted to sit next to him on the coach. As a result, my popularity was briefly elevated. I used to bring bags of sweets from my granddad's sweet emporium. You name it, I had it. Sherbet pips, fizzers, pick and mix, cola cubes, chewing nuts and black jacks were all packed inside my tiny brown leather satchel between the obligatory sandwiches, crisps and drink. I was generous too. I'd share them with all the other kids at very reasonable prices.

Now, at my school we had a trainee teacher called Mr Alfie Evans. We called him 'A & E' for short, as he was a walking casualty.

Since he was pretty useless at most things, I guess that's why he decided to try his hand at teaching kids who might not notice his inadequacies. But he underestimated us. Boy, was he hemmed in by his own incompetence.

I frequently ended up in his group. It was kind of a 'baptism of fire' for him because if he could survive with me for the day, then the other teachers thought he'd probably make it past Christmas.

Alfie Evans would take me and a few other misfits around the zoo and pretend to be knowledgeable. As you'd expect, we were not too interested in his talks. We were more interested in whether we could get the ostriches to eat bubble gum balls.

MR EVANS: Boys, there's a baby elephant.

WALTER: Oh really? I thought that was a penguin.

MR EVANS: No, I think you can tell by the trunk and flappy ears. Yes, it's an elephant. It says so here.

WALTER: Is it an African elephant or an Indian elephant?

MR EVANS: I don't know. Let me read this information board. No it was born here so I guess he's British.

WALTER: I don't like zoos anyway.

MR EVANS: Why not?

WALTER: I think the animals should be free and not kept in cages.

MR EVANS: Well, they can't just let them out because there are all these people here. They have to keep them locked up in case they hurt someone.

Most of us were not excited about elephants. We'd seen photos and television programmes and we knew you couldn't pick one up. What we loved was Pet's Corner. Let's face it, no one makes a documentary about gerbils or hamsters.

Pet's Corner gave us the opportunity to torment something that couldn't get away or put up a fight. We didn't mean to torment them but, after a day of continuous feeding, I guess you'd feel tormented if you had more food shoved into your mouth.

We all got to hold overweight, cute and furry things or feed baby goats and usually someone would try and smuggle something onto the coach. In those days we got searched, not for cigarettes or drugs but for rabbits, hamsters or guinea pigs. Sometimes the occasional concealed duck would give itself away as we drove out of the car park. Those were great days.

Fast forward now, some twenty years. I'm on a train with my son and several bags of traditional sweets, travelling to London Zoo. He's just four and a half and is naturally curious because he's never been on a train.

I'm thinking to myself, "I hope he doesn't say anything to embarrass me. He blurts out so much rubbish."

At that moment, a lady opposite leans over and starts talking to him.

What is it about women and small kids? Why do they have to talk to them? They don't feel the compulsion to talk to me – just kids. If you're a woman be warned by what happened next. Think twice before engaging in conversation with small children.

LADY: Hello, Little Boy. Where are you going today?

WALTER: *[Muttering]* Oh, no. Don't talk to him. He'll go on aimlessly for the whole journey because he thinks you want to be friends.

SON: London Zoo. I haven't been naughty. We're going to see the animals.

LADY: How lovely. Are you excited?

SON: *[To Walter]* Daddy, why is this lady so fat?

WALTER: I don't know. Why don't you ask her yourself? I don't want to get involved. I'm getting off at the next stop.

SON: *[To Lady]* Why are you so fat? Do you eat a lot? My daddy says people are fat because they are pigs.

WALTER: *[To Lady]* I'm so sorry. He doesn't mean to be rude. He doesn't always know what he's saying.

SON: I do! She's fat and I want to know if she's a pig!

We never went on a train again.

From an early age, Father often gave me
sweet cigarettes.

The Sweet Old Orange Lady

MIDGET GEM

LOUISE: Did you find everything you were looking for?

MRS ROBINSON: No. I can't find my husband.

I meet many old ladies in my shop. They all vie for attention and get very excited. Some are flirtatious but most are quite harmless. The members of the 'silver brigade' all have their special memories – they like to relive them and recount a multitude of stories to a captured audience – I just can't get away.

Though I'm chatted up on most occasions, my wife doesn't seem to care. As long as there's no pleasure in it for me, it's okay. While I gaze at the beautiful models who come in she will interrupt and remind them, "Next door's dog still chases after cars even though he doesn't know how to drive."

On one occasion I met, on first glance, a sweet old dear who'd just had an intense spray tan. She wanted to blend in with the young crowd at the beach although she would have blended in much better if she had opted to wear a 'hoodie'. Her name was Gladys.

GLADYS: Ooh hello. You washing the windows?

WALTER: Yes. That's what the bucket of soapy water's for. I also use it to scare creepy old ladies.

GLADYS: You can come and do mine, if you like?

WALTER: Not really.

GLADYS: *[Pinching Walter's bottom]* Then you can hoover my carpet!

WALTER: Get off! I don't want to hoover your carpet. I don't want to hoover anything. You old ladies are all the same. A few soft biscuits and a cup of lukewarm tea and you think you can have anyone.

GLADYS: Go on, walk me down your shop. Hold my arm.

WALTER: Oh, alright then.

[The pair walk down the shop and Walter quickly retreats behind the counter]

LOUISE: Another girlfriend then?

WALTER: She's my punishment.

GLADYS: That was lovely.

WALTER: The pleasure was all *yours*.

GLADYS: What a wonderful shop you have. So beautiful.

WALTER: You're too kind.

GLADYS: It reminds me of my childhood.

WALTER: *[To Louise]* Here we go again.

LOUISE: Don't be mean. She looks a sweet old lady.

WALTER: You mean *orange lady*. Not even the dim lighting can hide that.

GLADYS: When I was a little girl my brother used to share his mint imperials with me. I was only eight and that was ninety years ago.

LOUISE: Are you really ninety-eight?

GLADYS: Oh yes. Many say I look much younger.

WALTER: Never a day over eighty.

GLADYS: What a charmer you are. How old are you? I do like young men.

WALTER: Steady, tiger.

LOUISE: *[Laughing]* I don't think she takes prisoners.

GLADYS: But I've been known to tie a few men up.

WALTER: I don't want to know any more about your antics.

GLADYS: *[Leaning forward]* Give us a kiss!

WALTER: *[Stepping back]* She's like a ferocious gummy goldfish.

LOUISE: Have you been wearing that aftershave again, Walter?

WALTER: What, the one that attracts only old people?

LOUISE: Yes! What's it called?

WALTER: Formaldehyde.

LOUISE: *[Staring at Gladys]* Where did you get your tan from?

GLADYS: There's a new tanning shop opposite the café and they were offering discounts.

WALTER: I suspect they were using you to calibrate the machine. You are quite orange.

GLADYS: I know but I wanted to blend in with the younger crowd.

WALTER: You mean the ones in the Buddhist monastery?

GLADYS: No! The ones on the beach – you know?

LOUISE: He's just joking.

GLADYS: It took them hours to spray me.

LOUISE: But you're not that big?

WALTER: No, but think of all the folds and wrinkled areas they had to polyfill first.

GLADYS: Those are laugh lines. Very important if you want to get a man.

WALTER: Talking of getting things, what can we get you from our plethora of confectionary?

GLADYS: What's a plethora?

WALTER: It means *an overabundance*. Like your sex drive.

GLADYS: Cheeky! Oh, there's so much choice. I see you sell liquorice root.

LOUISE: Yes.

GLADYS: Excellent for constipation.

WALTER: You're meant to chew it, not use it as leverage.

GLADYS: Still, I don't need that at the moment. I've been up all night with a jippy tummy. I've just come back from Benidorm.

WALTER: Incontinent on the continent, eh? So you'll be going on the merry-go-round on the pier later?

GLADYS: Oh, no.

WALTER: Go on, go for gold!

GLADYS: It's more than gold they'll see if I go on one of those rides.

LOUISE: How about some liquorice comfits? Try one.

[Gladys takes a red one]

GLADYS: We used to use the red ones like lipstick. If you lick the end the colour comes off and then you can apply it.

[Gladys applies the red dye]

LOUISE: Doesn't she look beautiful, Walter?

WALTER: I'm not taking her out. I'm not safe.

LOUISE: You're not violent?

WALTER: No, I'm not safe from her.

LOUISE: *[To Gladys]* Maybe you'd like some nice old fashioned boiled sweets?

GLADYS: Yes. Can I have some of those orange and passion fruits? Emphasis on the passion!

WALTER: Although emphasis on the *orange* would be equally appropriate.

French Jedi Warriors

MIDGET GEM

> **BILL:** Can I have some American Hard Gums?
>
> **WALTER**: Sure. *Hard* gums for real men. None of those soft namby-pamby jellies for us.

The other day I had some unusual visitors. I say, 'unusual', because it's not often you meet a couple of French Jedi Warriors. Okay, they weren't really Jedi Warriors but their long gowns and hoods could have concealed a couple of light sabres.

At first they looked a bit sombre and not the type you'd employ as children's birthday party entertainers. However, first impressions, like marriage, can be misleading. One was carrying an oversized wooden paint easel while the other was struggling with a large picnic hamper weighed down by more than just sandwiches or crisps. As they moved closer and within range to become one of my targets, I took the opportunity to find out some more.

WALTER: Ah, Obi Wan. How are you?

BROTHER FRANCIS: Eh?

WALTER: What's with the fancy dress?

BROTHR FRANCIS: Oh I see. We're Trappist Monks on a day trip from France.

WALTER: So you're 'Day Trappers' then!

BROTHER JAQUES: Speech that leads to unkind amusement or laughter is seen as evil and is banned.

WALTER: Well, he's a bundle of laughs isn't he? He'll go down a storm in the local night club.

BROTHER FRANCIS: I'm sorry. He's a bit strict. He's very much into obedience and discipline.

LOUISE: I'm into discipline too.

WALTER: I've heard about that. Not too good at obedience though, are you? What will your wedding vows say? 'Love and obey if it doesn't mean I have to do as I am told.' I don't think he's into women.

BROTHER FRANCIS: On the contrary. We see women as a beautiful gift from God.

WALTER: You haven't met Louise, have you? She can change most people's view of women. Like 'pass-the-parcel', she's been around a few times but no one ever wants to unwrap a layer.

BROTHER FRANCIS: We would get married but our life of silence prevents us from asking a girl out.

WALTER: You don't have to ask Louise. She's usually right there in pursuit like a great white.

LOUISE: How do you communicate?

BROTHER FRANCIS: We use a secret ancient sign language. However, today is the one day of the year we can leave the monastery and experience life in the outside world. We're allowed to talk for twenty-four hours on any subject.

WALTER: This could be interesting. I would ask Louise what she'd talk about for a day if she had to be silent for a year but that sort of hypothetical question is just too hypothetical.

BROTHER FRANCIS: We're also giving away copies of our new CD.

WALTER: Don't tell me. Two hours of complete silence. Men can put it on and when their wives start moaning they can say, "Do you mind? I'm listening to this."

BROTHER FRANCIS: No, it's chanting and meditation.

WALTER: No wonder you're giving it away. Mind you, my wife is quite religious.

BROTHER FRANCIS: Really?

WALTER: Yes. When we're out together she often prays.

BROTHER FRANCIS: That's wonderful! What does she pray?

WALTER: Usually I hear her say things like, "Lord, give me strength."

LOUISE: So since today is a special day what shall we talk about?

BROTHER FRANCIS: I don't know. I like growing carrots and turnips. Do you like gardening, Louise?

LOUISE: Not really. Your habits – what do you wear under them?

BROTHER FRANCIS: Not much.

BROTHER JAQUES: Nothing at all.

BROTHER FRANCIS: What? I signed to you yesterday that we need pants as we were going out.

BROTHER JAQUES: Did you? When?

BROTHER FRANCIS: At the vegetable plot in the afternoon.

BROTHER JAQUES: Oh, I thought you were signing, 'Paints'. I brought a whole set of water colours.

BROTHER FRANCIS: I wondered why you were struggling to take that enormous easel on board the ferry.

LOUISE: What's the food like back home?

BROTHER FRANCIS: Oh, it's awful.

LOUISE: Why don't you say something?

BROTHER JAQUES: Because they haven't taught us how to complain in sign language.

WALTER: I know how to complain using just two fingers. Shall I show you?

LOUISE: No, don't. They'll get in awful trouble.

WALTER: Yes, I can see it now. Angry hands frantically signing between the head monk and these two. It'd be like the 'Gunfight at the OK Corral' with water pistols.

LOUISE: What are your rooms like?

WALTER: They don't live in a hotel, woman. These are sheltered folk.

LOUISE: You mean they live in sheltered housing?

WALTER: No. They're sheltered safely away from people like you!

BROTHER FRANCIS: We live in a commune. Each of us has his own cell.

LOUISE: Like working here then?

BROTHER FRANCIS: It's not too bad. We thrive on the tranquility and learning the monastery offers. I wasn't always a monk. I woke up one day and just knew I had to get away.

LOUISE: I feel like that most days.

WALTER: What did you do before?

BROTHER FRANCIS: If I told you that I might have to kill you.

WALTER: *[With a wry smile across to Louise]* Can you tell Louise?

LOUISE: Ha ha. Very funny. Not.

BROTHER JAQUES: His work was *top* secret.

WALTER: Really?

LOUISE: How exciting!

BROTHER FRANCIS: I was a field agent. I travelled the world – guns, cars, beautiful women – I got none of them.

WALTER: Why?

BROTHER JAQUES: He was an agriculturalist for the French government investigating the risks posed by GM crops.

BROTHER FRANCIS: Why don't you tell them what you used to do?

BROTHER JAQUES: I don't want to.

BROTHER FRANCIS: Well I do. And I will! He was a *Penguinologist*.

WALTER: Free chocolate biscuits then?

BROTHER FRANCIS: Yes! And we always waddle into dinner just to annoy him.

LOUISE: So now you've left those exciting careers, what do you do for fun?

BROTHER JAQUES: Contemplation.

BROTHER FRANCIS: Gardening.

BROTHER JAQUES: Meditation.

BROTHER FRANCIS: Painting.

LOUISE: Ooh, you're creative? I'm creative.

WALTER: Creative? You? The only time you're creative is when you make excuses for arriving late to work.

BROTHER JAQUES: Reading.

BROTHER FRANCIS: Brewing beer.

WALTER: Beer?

BROTHER FRANCIS: Yes. It's the one thing we're allowed. We brew some of the world's finest beer.

LOUISE: Party!

BROTHER JAQUES: Partying is seen as evil and is banned.

BROTHER FRANCIS: We also produce cheese, bread, clothing and large polished wooden boxes.

LOUISE: Boxes? We need some storage boxes.

BROTHER FRANCIS: I don't think they'd be very appropriate.

LOUISE: Why?

BROTHER FRANCIS: They're an odd shape.

LOUISE: We've got some odd shaped things to store. They'd be really useful.

BROTHER FRANCIS: You wouldn't like them.

LOUISE: I'm sure we would.

BROTHER FRANCIS: They're coffins.

WALTER: He's right, we wouldn't like them.

LOUISE: How many men are at the monastery?

BROTHER FRANCIS: About three hundred.

LOUISE: Can I come back with you?

WALTER: Don't take her. It'd be like letting a fox loose in a chicken house. They'd stand no chance.

BROTHER JAQUES: Brother Francis, we need to go soon or we'll miss our fish and chip lunch with Brother Jean and Brother Bob.

WALTER: Brother Bob?

BROTHER JAQUES: He's from Bognor. Brother Francis, we need to go.

BROTHER FRANCIS: But I want some sweets.

LOUISE: Sweets aren't seen as evil and are banned then?

BROTHER FRANCIS: No, they're okay. What do you recommend?

WALTER: Well, Jedi Warriors, may I suggest these old fashioned favourites? Flying saucers – they're out of this world.

BROTHER FRANCIS: Oh yes, I haven't had those for years.

BROTHER JAQUES: But Brother Francis, we haven't any money.

WALTER: How about some of that beer?

BROTHER FRANCIS: Yes I've got some of that in my basket. I've only got large bottles.

WALTER: *[Grinning in anticipation]* That will do nicely. Here's an extra-large bag of sweets in exchange.

BROTHER FRANCIS: Be careful, it's very strong.

Later that day…

LOUISE: Where are you, Walter?

WALTER: I'm down here.

LOUISE: Where? In the cellar?

WALTER: I'm under the table, my beautiful assistant.

LOUISE: That stuff really is strong.

Police, Camera, No Action!

MIDGET GEM

> **MRS HENDERSON:** Have you got any Army and Navy?
>
> **WALTER**: Oh yes. You ladies just can't resist a sweet in a uniform.

You'd think the local constabulary would make you feel safe, right? Wrong. They make everyone feel guilty. Just think for a moment back to the last time you saw a policeman coming towards you in the street. Okay, you might say it was quite a long time ago but I bet anything you felt nervous.

I've got to tell you something. Every time the police come in my shop they clear the place. Either my customers are all crooks or everyone has just remembered they need to pay their car tax. I can't help but notice how young they look. In fact, I wonder where their parents are.

However, they always get a friendly welcome. There has become a large following for and frequent purchase of sweet beer bottles by the local force. Ironic, isn't it? However, I wish I could receive the same welcome and efficient service when I visit their premises.

The other week I had a shoplifter in - one of my regulars. He cleared my shelf of toffee slabs and I ran after him. It was like something from a 'Laurel and Hardy' film. Even an old lady in a white mini stopped and said, "I think he went down Salisbury Road!" She didn't offer to pursue him for me and he escaped. Fortunately I wasn't far from the police station and I decided to report the incident.

These police stations are fortresses aren't they? It took me twenty minutes to get inside once I'd passed the security checks. At least the policemen are safe. I approached the desk and was, at first, ignored by the school kid on duty. I rang the bell and waited.

WALTER: Excuse me! Are you going to help me or are you more interested in watering the begonia plants?

PC STEVENS: There's no need to take that tone with me. If I don't water these plants they'll suffer.

WALTER: I'm suffering.

PC STEVENS: Really, Sir? Would you like some water?

WALTER: No, I don't want any water.

PC STEVENS: What can I do for you?

WALTER: I want to report some shoplifting.

PC STEVENS: What did you take?

WALTER: Nothing! I want to report some theft of items from *my* shop.

PC STEVENS: I see. I suppose I can take a few details. But if the phone rings I'll have to answer it.

WALTER: Why?

PC STEVENS: I'm waiting for an important call back.

WALTER: So what do you need to know?

PC STEVENS: Perhaps your name first, Sir.

WALTER: Walter Jones.

[The telephone rings]

PC STEVENS: I'll have to get this.

WALTER: What a surprise.

PC STEVENS: Hello. Oh, I'm glad you phoned back. We'd like number 27, 49, 52a and 84. Do you do any of those sesame seed toasts? Lovely – add those on then. Free prawn crackers? Brilliant. I'll get one of our cars out to collect it all in about fifteen minutes. Thanks, Mr Chan.

WALTER: What's going on? Can we get on with the report?

[Just then the sergeant comes out from the back room]

SERGEANT: Everything alright, Sir? You look a bit harassed?

WALTER: Since when has ordering lunch taken priority over my crime report?

SERGEANT: Don't be too harsh. He's new. Next time he'll order it much quicker. *[To PC Stevens]* It's your turn for darts. Simon's got 204 and you need 83 to win. Off you go.

PC STEVENS: I'll be there in a minute. I just need to finish watering these plants. Can you send a car to Mr Chan's? Food will be ready in fifteen.

SERGEANT: Crikey, that's not long. We'll have to put the sirens and lights on.

WALTER: Perhaps you'd like to send someone around to me?

SERGEANT: We are a bit short staffed, Sir. What with lunch and that.

WALTER: Unbelievable. What do you want me to do? Catch the criminal myself and bring him in here for you?

SERGEANT: Don't bring him in here, whatever you do. We try to keep criminals out of here. The lads get upset with all the bad language. They're very sensitive recruits these days.

WALTER: I'm sensitive about having stuff pinched from my shop.

SERGEANT: What did he take?

WALTER: All my toffee slabs with the metal hammers inside.

SERGEANT: Hammers, Sir? Are you stocking offensive weapons? You need a licence!

WALTER: No, the hammers are used to break the toffee into small bits.

SERGEANT: Or to hack into someone's skull!

WALTER: They are only three inches long.

SERGEANT: That's no excuse to stock vicious illegal weapons.

WALTER: I frequently see old ladies use their handbags as vicious weapons on their husbands but I don't see any arrests reported in the local paper.

SERGEANT: That's different.

WALTER: Why?

SERGEANT: Old ladies remind me of my grandmother. Sweet old dear.

WALTER: Listen, I'm a victim of crime. What are you going to do about it?

SERGEANT: Look, stop feeling sorry for yourself. Get some counselling and move on.

WALTER: I want you to catch the crook.

SERGEANT: We're about to have lunch. Can't it wait?

WALTER: No it can't! Look, I've written a description down from the CCTV.

[Walter passes over a piece of paper]

SERGEANT: Ah. Yes. Blue jeans, camouflage top. Might be difficult to find him if he has a camouflage top. What's he camouflaged as?

WALTER: A zebra.

SERGEANT: Well, if he goes in the zoo we've lost him.

WALTER: No, I was joking. He's wearing an army type camouflage jacket.

SERGEANT: I see. Black beard, hooked nose, pink framed glasses. Could be anyone.

WALTER: He's got a scar across his forehead.

SERGEANT: Why? Did you assault him, Sir? That's an offence.

WALTER: No. It looks like it's been there for ages. I chased him off.

SERGEANT: You do realise that if he falls over and grazes his knee he is quite entitled to press charges against you?

WALTER: What's the point in talking to you? This is useless. Next time your lads come into the shop and ask for sweet beer bottles don't blame me when they come back empty handed because he took those too.

SERGEANT: He took all the sweet beer bottles?

WALTER: Yes. Every last one.

[The sergeant dashes over to the other side of the office and opens the door leading to the darts room]

SERGEANT: Here, lads! Take six squad cars and scour the streets. Be on the lookout for a hooked nosed bearded individual with pink glasses and a camouflage jacket. He's in possession of our sweet beer bottles.

[The sergeant returns to Walter as twelve policemen bundle through the reception]

SERGEANT: Don't you worry, Sir. We'll get him.

Dish It With Denise

MIDGET GEM

MISS DICKENSON: Have you got aniseed balls?

WALTER: No. But I hear it's a terrible affliction.

Louise is not the most diligent of employees. In fact, she needs to be motivated quite often using various techniques. My favourite involves a cattle prod.

If she's not eyeing up the young men then she's either doing her nails or reading a magazine. One morning I caught her doing next to nothing. I think the correct phrase is, 'sod all'. She was leaning on the counter intently reading something.

WALTER: What are you reading?

LOUISE: A girly magazine.

WALTER: Why?

LOUISE: It's quiet and I've finished all my other jobs.

WALTER: What jobs?

LOUISE: My nails and hair.

WALTER: Give me that magazine.

LOUISE: But I'm reading the self-help letters.

WALTER: You've always helped yourself to most things. *Especially* men. What's the column called?

LOUISE: 'Dish It With Denise'.

WALTER: 'Dish It With Denise'?

LOUISE: Yes. You send her a letter stating your problem and she suggests an answer.

WALTER: Oh, it's one of *those* sorts of columns is it? They're just an excuse to complain about the opposite sex. It may as well be called, 'Moan About Men'.

LOUISE: Denise is very good.

WALTER: Come on. Hand it over. I want to take a look.

[Louise hands the magazine over and Walter reviews the column]

WALTER: It's very thumbed, this magazine. I bet you relish all the gossip and lies in here.

LOUISE: It's a healthy distraction from you.

WALTER: Look at this letter and her response!

LOUISE: Which one?

WALTER: I'll read it to you.

DISH IT WITH DENISE

Your self-help guide to serious domestic problems

Dear Denise,

My husband won't help out around the house. I think he's a lazy bone-idle good-for-nothing. What do you think I should do?

Yours hopingly,

Jane of Northampton

DENISE SAYS:

Dear Jane,

My heart goes out to you, pet.

All men are lazy bone-idle good-for-nothings. It's a well-known fact.

Now listen, pet. You're not alone but this is a problem that won't go away unless you get help. Some women have tried new lingerie to get their husband's attention but that only makes a man anxious because men can never live up to expectations. Many women have written in about their love lives and frequently summarise it with the words, "Is that it?" So lingerie is not the answer.

No. You need to get a few of your friends, about three, to support you through this terrible crisis. Ask them to pop in for coffee and when you're all together they can encourage you by giving your husband several hard slaps across his face and telling him to get off his back side. They need to humiliate him as much as possible.

Good luck, pet, and remember you can always call the helpline if you need more women to come round your house and join in.

Denise

LOUISE: She's very good, isn't she? She understands real issues and problems and has a unique insight to solving them.

WALTER: Since when has humiliating men been a new thing?

LOUISE: But she has an approach many women haven't tried yet. Group support is a new concept against the tide of male apathy.

WALTER: Well, I'm glad my wife doesn't fill her head with this rubbish. Look at this front cover article. 'What does it feel like when everyone sees you naked?'

LOUISE: It's an interesting article.

WALTER: It's trash. I can tell you what it feels like.

LOUISE: Really?

WALTER: Yes. Some kids took my swimming trunks and towel at the swimming pool and I had to get out in front of everyone. It was a gala day and all the spectator seats were filled. And I didn't like what the policeman did with his truncheon either. It still smarts today.

LOUISE: Ha ha. Serves you right.

WALTER: Here, you can have this rubbish back.

[Louise continues to read the self-help pages.]

LOUISE: Have you read the last letter?

WALTER: No. Why?

LOUISE: Now this is interesting. I'll read it to you.

DISH IT WITH DENISE

Your self-help guide to serious domestic problems

Dear Denise,

My husband runs a sweet shop but doesn't want to go shopping with me. He's happy to work in a shop but won't go in any others. We've been married nearly twenty-five years.

What should I do?

Yours unhappily,

Mrs Jones of Sussex

DENISE SAYS:

Dear Mrs Jones,

Oh, pet, you must be suffering awfully with a dolt of a husband like that. It sounds to me that he's mean spirited, ungenerous, ungrateful and thoughtless to the one person who's loved and slaved away for him most of her adult life.

Now, whatever you do, pet, don't try and understand him because you could end up giving him excuses. He's clearly wrong because he's a man.

He's probably bad at conversation too so it's not worth talking to him about it either.

Sometimes, when you're married to such a terrible man, it can be a blessing to go shopping on your own. You can buy what you like and not tell him. Spend as much of his money as you can and shower yourself with gifts because you're worth it. You'll probably find that as the bank balance goes down he'll want to go with you more often.

Good luck, pet, and remember you can always call the helpline because there are women here who know how to extract more shopping money from their husband's bank account.

Denise

Fit and Healthy

MIDGET GEM

> **MARJORIE:** Have you got cherry lips?
>
> **WALTER**: No. I always look like this.

Doctors are a strange breed. It's been my observation that's driven me to the conclusion that they have the answers to many problems, provided it involves the application of some unpleasant ointment or medicine that has such awful side effects. I am, of course, referring to *their* problems, not ours. By prescribing some foul tasting, personality changing concoction or pain inflicting, corrosive haemorrhoid cream we are less likely to go back. This helps them to reach targets and reduce waiting times. The next time you go in with a sprained ankle just see if your doctor leaves a chain saw out on his desk to unnerve you.

Humiliation is another tactic. The last time I went to the surgery my doctor asked me to get down on all fours in the corner of the room. When I enquired as to the reason the reply was, "Well, I'm thinking of buying a coffee table and I wanted to see what it might look like over there."

My doctor frequently complains about my shop. "Sweets are bad for you and cause obesity." is the usual rhetoric. I think that's rich coming from someone who smokes a pipe on a regular basis. Many's the time my doctor has been seen emptying a pipe out against the heel of a shoe and refilling it with a large wad of tobacco. Lighting up with a match and puffing away, any public space soon becomes a fog infested moor. I've told her she should give it up.

She ordered me the other day to lose weight. "Have you tried Granola?" she asked.

"I don't like German girls." I replied.

She then told me to start exercising. But I do exercise! Frequently! At least four times a week I take up running. Yes, running. Running away from old ladies. Sometimes it becomes a marathon. You might think they're slow but don't be deceived. Quite often they set off at half speed and just when you think you've got away they have a final burst and catch up. And then there's the shoplifters. With few police around, I am left with no alternative but to set off in pursuit. Most are younger and get away but I do manage to catch some. As I put my hand on their shoulder and say, "Come with me!" they turn around to reveal that they're a toothless old lady wanting to be caught. And boy, are they up for coming with me. In shock and obvious disgust I let go of them as quickly as possible and a reverse chase ensues. Those oldies are crafty.

Talking of exercise, I have a personal trainer who comes in the shop. He's not *my* personal trainer, of course. He's too handsome and fit. He once told me he likes to oil up his body in the morning so I offered him a spare can of 'Three-In-One'. While he jogs about in the shop and pretends to stretch his muscles, he takes delight in giving me advice. Advice such as, "It's never too late. You're never too old to start." Start what? A fight? How old do I look? Who wants to work their way to a coronary? Who is he kidding when he exclaims, "You don't want to die unhealthy!" I don't want to die, full stop. What has health got to do with it? Most people die because of poor health. It's natural. The very act of dying says you're not well. As long as I can escape the elderly then that's good enough for me. I don't need a six pack or rippling muscles. I can't cope with the attention I get now, let alone with what I'd get if I was even *more* handsome. Beauty is skin deep and I tell that to every old dragon that comes into the shop.

I'm not one of those '10 miles a day' types. More like 10 yards. But that's okay. Mrs Jones is not asking me to run far (at the moment). In fact, she has her own methods of getting me out of the house when she wants a bit of peace and quiet. And I'm happy to go. I think these personal trainers are just after our money or to make us feel bad. We all seem to think we can end up looking like them – so slim, handsome or beautiful (depending on whether he's wearing makeup). Actually, the adverts I see for personal trainers always picture a beautiful twenty-five year old woman. "Come and train with Emma." they invite. Who are they kidding? That's not her photo. Or, if it is, it was her photo thirty years ago. She's there to lure you in. What you actually end up with contravenes trading standards!

No, I think I'll carry on eating my favourite sweets and running away from old ladies. There's no point getting on a cycle machine and peddling thirty miles to allow me to eat a chocolate bar (small one at that). Laughter is the best cure. When I think of all those unhappy, depressed people in the doctor's surgery (most of them *are* the doctors from the surgery) I realize how lucky I am. Stay away from doctors – you're doing yourself and them a great service.

Mr Cool

MIDGET GEM

MR HUGHES: I love toffee.

WALTER: I love tea. I love the java jive and it loves me. Coffee and tea and the jiving and me. A cup a cup a cup a cup a cup!

MR HUGHES: Toffee! Not Coffee! You're a bounder and a scallywag!

He was the coolest man I've ever met. I use the word 'cool' in a profoundly different sense from the way kids use it to describe the latest gadget or song. To me, 'cool' is not something you can try to be. Trying to be 'cool' just displays some egotistical flaw that results in everyone around you reaching the conclusion that you're probably just an idiot.

No, this guy was cool. He's the sort of guy people aspire to be but can't. He wasn't trying to be cool - he just was cool. It was in his nature.

He breezed into the shop wearing expensive motorbike leathers and spent the first few minutes browsing. I could see Louise was quaking at the knees and she already had her pen and paper ready for his telephone number. Like a foaming rabid dog, she was going to grab whatever she could.

MR COOL: Nice shop.

WALTER: Why, thank you. I thought…

LOUISE: *[Interrupts]* Hellooo. I'm Louise.

MR COOL: Hello Louise.

LOUISE: My, aren't you tall?

MR COOL: Yeah, I was being careful not to damage your Victorian hanging lamps.

LOUISE: Oh, I wouldn't worry about them. And you can always sue old fish face if you bang your head.

WALTER: Eh?

MR COOL: I'll try not to walk into one.

LOUISE: Have you travelled far to get here? I've been all around the world and just love to meet fellow travellers.

WALTER: *[Looking at Louise]* I can see your game. This is a sweet shop, not a dating agency.

MR COOL: Yes, I've been around a bit.

WALTER: So's she.

MR COOL: Actually I'm off on a bike trip across the USA.

LOUISE: Wow! How exciting. I do like all your badges.

MR COOL: Thank you. Each one tells a story.

WALTER: I bet. Does the 'AA' badge tell about the time you broke down? Or is it Alcoholics Anonymous?

LOUISE: *[Turning to Walter]* Shush!

MR COOL: Actually, 'AA' stands for 'Africa Aid'. I try to help out where I can.

LOUISE: How wonderful.

WALTER: Bloody do-gooder. It can't get any worse.

MR COOL: Well, I think I'll take one of these treacle toffee slabs.

LOUISE: Ooh, would you like me to unwrap it for you?

WALTER: Stop drivelling, girl. Just let him go.

LOUISE: What do you do when you're not on your motorbike?

MR COOL: Well, I'm not sure I want to say.

LOUISE: Oh, go on!

WALTER: *[Under his breath]* Yeah, go on. Make me feel even smaller while you muscle in on my staff.

MR COOL: I'm a dentist.

LOUISE: Really? You can examine my teeth any time.

WALTER: What? Examine your teeth? Everyone can see your teeth! Bloody Jaws look-a-like!

MR COOL: Yeah. I practice in a small village but I'm taking six months out to bike across the States with my receptionist. Here she comes now.

RECEPTIONIST: *[Kisses Mr cool]* Hi darling. Are you ready to go?

MR COOL: Yes, sweetie. *[Turning to Louise]* How much do I owe you?

WALTER: *[Interrupts]* No, no. Nothing at all. Have this on me.

MR COOL: Why, thank you. See you all when I get back.

WALTER: *[Grinning at a disappointed Louise]* Bye. It's been a real pleasure.

LOUISE: *[Glaring at the couple as they leave]* I hate her. She's a slut.

The Rubbish Magician

MIDGET GEM

> **WALTER**: What's red, hard and bad for your teeth?
>
> **AWKWARD CUSTOMER**: I don't know.
>
> **WALTER**: A brick

Why is it that people think that my shop is an audition studio? Most weeks I'm forced to endure a new act performed by someone so naturally incompetent. They are all unique in their own way – no one else could be so bad at their act even with their best endeavours.

There was the Sussex Snake Charmer, who totally lost control of his animals and cleared the shop in two minutes. His antics caused such a panic in the town that the authorities introduced new measures banning the public carrying of wicker baskets.

The Swiss Sword Swallower's sabre got so stuck half way down that even a passing member of St John's Ambulance looked in, abandoned all hope and just kept walking.

And what about Brighton's Biggest Wrestler? He spent forty-five minutes lodged in the doorway despite numerous prods from a pensioner with an umbrella. She wanted her weekly ration of acid drops and he was the only thing between her and them. There were ugly scenes and he left in tears. Never stop a pensioner on the path to their bag of sweets.

And then there's George. He calls himself, 'Marvin the Magician' because some idiot gave him a kid's magic set for his birthday. His outstandingly bad performances are further lowered to the depths due to his poor hearing and very short memory. I remember a particularly tough day. Louise had just returned from a scouting week in Magaluf. "Scouting?" you ask. Yes, 'scouting for men'.

WALTER: So you're back then?

LOUISE: Yes.

WALTER: They let you in okay?

LOUISE: What do you mean?

WALTER: Well, aren't you getting a bit old for this 'Magaluf' party business?

LOUISE: No. I'm still in my twenties.

WALTER: And still resisting any advance to thirty? It will happen. There's no point in denying it. You're doomed. Like sour milk you will turn thirty.

LOUISE: Well, that day hasn't arrived and I'm still partying. Have you booked your SAGA holiday? Send A Granddad Abroad.

WALTER: I don't qualify.

LOUISE: *[Whispers across menacingly]* Too old.

WALTER: What was that? I've still got it, you know.

LOUISE: Pity you can't remember what to do with it.

WALTER: You're shameless.

LOUISE: I know! Isn't it fun? I met a new man on holiday.

WALTER: He won't be new for much longer, then. Still, I guess that means the rest of the male population is safe for another day or two.

LOUISE: Don't be rude. He's coming round later.

WALTER: Why? Is he unconscious? What have you done to him?

LOUISE: No, he's coming round later for dinner.

WALTER: Don't tell me you're cooking for the poor sod?

LOUISE: Yes. Why?

WALTER: Because that's bad. You're the only woman I know who has ever burnt a fresh fruit salad. Few people ever go on to live normal lives after sampling your cooking. What are you attempting this time?

LOUISE: Lasagne.

WALTER: *[Astonished]* Lasagne? That sounds like a good choice.

LOUISE: With anchovies.

WALTER: Not so good. Why aren't you using mince like everyone else?

LOUISE: Anchovies were on offer.

WALTER: I won't give him long in your flat. One bite and he'll be gone.

LOUISE: The dinner won't be that bad!

WALTER: No. One bite from *you* and he'll be gone. You know how desperate you get when you're alone with a man. Every time you go on holiday you bring someone back. Who was it last time?

LOUISE: Michael.

WALTER: Yes. You went to Fray Bentos, didn't you?

LOUISE: That's a meat packager!

WALTER: Exactly. You'll have a tin of anything you can lay your hands on. Why don't you just wait for love to arrive?

LOUISE: Have you seen what arrives on the 9.30 from Reading?

WALTER: Yes, I see what you mean.

[Louise looks around the shop for empty shelves to restock]

LOUISE: The shop looks tidy. Didn't you sell much while I was away?

WALTER: I've had a nightmare of a week. For the last seven days I've had Marvin the Magician in.

LOUISE: That must have been fun?

WALTER: No, he's rubbish. And he's not called Marvin. His real name is George. And he's no magician. He's a retired water board official.

LOUISE: How bad is he?

WALTER: Well, put it this way - even his pet rabbit doesn't want to join in.

THE RUBBISH MAGICIAN 69

[Just then, Marvin walks into the shop brandishing a pack of playing cards]

WALTER: *[To Louise]* Oh no, here he is again.

MARVIN: Hello, Sir. My name is Marvin the Magician.

WALTER: Hello, George.

MARVIN: No, it's Marvin!

LOUISE: *[Looking at Walter, sternly]* Play the game.

WALTER: Hello, Marvin.

MARVIN: I'm going to show you a trick that will astound you.

WALTER: *[To Louise]* I'll be astounded if he manages to pull it off.

MARVIN: Pick a card, any card!

WALTER: *[To Louise]* Not this one again. We've never got to the end of it.

LOUISE: Why?

WALTER: He can't remember it. You have to try and help him.

LOUISE: How?

WALTER: By calling the authorities.

MARVIN: Pick a card, any card!

WALTER: *[To Marvin]* Okay, I'll take this one.

MARVIN: Lovely. Now look at it and don't show me what it is.

WALTER: *[To Louise]* I don't have to look at it. It's the ace of spades. It's always the ace of spades. It's never anything else. He's got a whole pack full of the ace of spades. I'd like to give him a spade.

MARVIN: Have you looked at it?

WALTER: Yes.

MARVIN: Jolly good. [Pauses a moment] Pick a card, any card!

WALTER: *[To Marvin]* We've done that bit.

MARVIN: What?

WALTER: I've already picked a card.

MARVIN: Oh, sorry. Now look at it and don't show me what it is.

WALTER: I've done that bit too.

MARVIN: What?

WALTER: I've done that already.

MARVIN: Done what?

WALTER: Looked at the card.

MARVIN: When?

WALTER: Just now.

MARVIN: Okay. Have you got any scissors?

WALTER: Yes.

MARVIN: I want you to cut the card into small pieces.

LOUISE: Here's some scissors. *[Hands the scissors to Walter]*

MARVIN: *[Looking very worried]* What are you doing with those?

WALTER: I'm going to cut the card up.

MARVIN: Why?

WALTER: You told me to.

MARVIN: Why?

WALTER: It's part of the trick.

MARVIN: What trick?

WALTER: The card trick you were showing me.

MARVIN: You can't cut that up!

WALTER: Why?

MARVIN: I haven't got enough to last the week. Here, take these bits and pretend. *[Marvin gathers some pieces of card from a trouser pocket]*

WALTER: *[To Louise]* This is a rubbish trick.

LOUISE: And you had this going on all last week?

WALTER: Mornings and afternoons.

LOUISE: Ha ha.

MARVIN: *[Scratching his head]* Pick a card, any card!

WALTER: *[To Louise]* I'd pay real money if he'd just go away. *[To Marvin]* I've got a card already and we've pretended to cut it up.

MARVIN: *[Produces a brown envelope]* I want you to put the pieces in this envelope.

WALTER: It's sealed. That's your electric bill.

MARVIN: *[Produces another envelope]* How about this one?

WALTER: That's your gas bill. Here, I've got an envelope. Will that do?

MARVIN: Is it a magic one?

WALTER: Like the utility bill ones – they always manage to find you, don't they? Yes it's magic.

LOUISE: Is it?

WALTER: *[Whispering]* No you idiot. I got from the pound shop.

MARVIN: Okay. Put the pieces in there.

WALTER: Here we are. All in the envelope. *[Hands the envelope to Marvin]* What shall I do with this card?

MARVIN: *[Amazed]* Where did you get that from?

WALTER: The pack.

MARVIN: When did you do that? I didn't see you. Can you show me how you did it? You've got a very good sleight of hand.

WALTER: You're meant to tell me what my card is and produce another one.

MARVIN: But I don't know what your card is?

WALTER: *[Holding up the card]* It's the ace of spades.

MARVIN: How did you do that? You guessed my card!

WALTER: No, it was my card.

MARVIN: *[Pauses]* Pick a card, any card!

WALTER: *[Looking despairingly at Louise]* Do you want to endure two hours of this? It will be like watching a repeat of your least favourite program with a rewind to the worst bits.

LOUISE: Not really.

WALTER: *[To Marvin]* Marvin, how ever do you do it? You guessed my card again! You're a genius.

MARVIN: I am?

WALTER: What a brilliant magician you are.

MARVIN: *[Smiling]* Thank you. It takes me so long to learn a new trick. I quite often forget things.

WALTER: That's okay. Would you like your usual sweets today?

MARVIN: *[Looking very sad]* Oh dear.

LOUISE: What's the matter, Marvin?

MARVIN: I can't remember what I usually have.

WALTER: It's okay, George. I'll do the remembering for you. You always buy these liquorice wands.

MARVIN: I love those. How did you know?

WALTER: Magic!

MARVIN: *[Pays for his sweets]* Thank you. You've made my day. These bring back wonderful memories. Goodbye.

WALTER: Bye for now.

[Marvin leaves the shop]

LOUISE: *[Bemused]* You were very kind to him. Why?

WALTER: He's fading away but sometimes all he needs is someone to bring him back. I doubt he'll remember me but those sweets will conjure up some happier times.

Marvin was such a bad magician that even his pet rabbit didn't want to join in.

Do It Yourself

MIDGET GEM

> **MR SMITH:** I haven't seen any Fishermen's Friends in your shop?
>
> **WALTER**: No, but you have just passed one of their enemies.

I guess I pride myself in the unique service my shop offers. Nowhere else can you be made to feel special, helped or insulted without measure. We don't feel constrained by political correctness or shackled by personal etiquette. Nope. We're free and uncompromising in our dynamic and unique approach to customer care.

Furthermore, you'll never hear us say, "Have a nice day." Yuck!

"Have a great day! Unless you've got other plans." is a far better alternative.

Now don't get me wrong. I know the other establishments try their best. I know they mean well. Yet it irritates me that some have adopted a new type of customer service. This is especially true of those huge stores offering everything from cushions to serrated knives, dining ornaments to power saws or pretty bathroom blinds to deadly shears. Louise is obviously fond of these places but I have found that they cultivate a deep dislike when it comes to the checkout process.

What happened to the sweet girl with braces who'd smile nervously as you carried through a chainsaw and set of pliers? I've always enjoyed intimidating them. They've taken DIY too far. "We sell DIY and now you can checkout DIY style." Listen, I didn't apply to be a 'checkout chick'. I'm useless at it and if I'm wearing the wrong glasses then I've no hope of finding the hidden bar code. Not content with that, they've implemented talking checkout machines! I was so traumatised by my last visit that the following evening I had a nightmare. I was tentatively approaching the checkout…

WALTER: Now where the hell is everyone? What am I meant to do here?

CHECKOUT MACHINE: Ooh Hello!

WALTER: What? Who said that?

CHECKOUT MACHINE: I did, luvvie.

WALTER: Who?

CHECKOUT MACHINE: Me. I'm your checkout assistant machine. I'm here to help you.

WALTER: Huh! Where's a real person?

CHECKOUT MACHINE: I have a real person's voice.

WALTER: Very camp it is too.

CHECKOUT MACHINE: Ooooh! Aren't we cheeky today!

WALTER: Look, I want to get out of here.

CHECKOUT MACHINE: Not without paying first.

WALTER: I know. What do I do?

CHECKOUT MACHINE: Touch my screen.

WALTER: I beg your pardon?

CHECKOUT MACHINE: Touch my screen. You know you want to.

WALTER: Get off.

CHECKOUT MACHINE: Touch my screen where it says, 'Start'.

WALTER: *[Touches the screen]* Don't get me started. There.

CHECKOUT MACHINE: You've got such a gentle touch. You're obviously a delicate and sensitive man.

WALTER: Nothing's happening.

CHECKOUT MACHINE: Maybe not at your end but I'm enjoying it.

WALTER: Nothing's happening to your screen.

CHECKOUT MACHINE: You need to be a bit more forceful, love. Go on, touch me again.

WALTER: You're making me feel very uncomfortable now.

CHECKOUT MACHINE: Go on. I'm looking forward to it!

WALTER: *[Touches the screen]* There.

CHECKOUT MACHINE: Alright! There's no need to poke me so hard! I've got feelings.

WALTER: I bet you have.

CHECKOUT MACHINE: I'm not going to help you if you're rude to me. I shall sit here until you apologise.

WALTER: I want to go home. Oh, come on? Alright, I'm sorry.

CHECKOUT MACHINE: Sorry with a cherry on top?

WALTER: Don't push your luck.

CHECKOUT MACHINE: Okay. All you need to do is scan each item by flashing the barcode over my window. This will be fun.

WALTER: Why?

CHECKOUT MACHINE: It tickles.

WALTER: I'm really beginning to feel uneasy talking to you.

CHECKOUT MACHINE: Go on, scan something.

WALTER: There.

CHECKOUT MACHINE: Beep. Ooh, a set of paint brushes. You went for the cheap ones then?

WALTER: So what?

CHECKOUT MACHINE: You'll regret it. You get what you pay for.

WALTER: They're fine.

CHECKOUT MACHINE: Cheapskate.

WALTER: I am not!

CHECKOUT MACHINE: Bet you're rubbish at painting anyway.

WALTER: Can we get on?

CHECKOUT MACHINE: We are in a grumpy mood, aren't we?

WALTER: Here's the next item.

CHECKOUT MACHINE: Beep. Pink paint?

WALTER: My wife's choice.

CHECKOUT MACHINE: Don't be shy. We all understand.

WALTER: I am *not* gay.

CHECKOUT MACHINE: We can announce it over the tannoy if you like? We can call you, 'The Pink Painter'.

WALTER: No.

CHECKOUT MACHINE: You'll have to come out sometime.

WALTER: Next item!

CHECKOUT MACHINE: Beep. A step ladder. You be careful with that. Old people should always have someone to help them to avoid heights.

WALTER: I'm not old.

CHECKOUT MACHINE: You're no spring chicken.

WALTER: Who asked you? Next item.

CHECKOUT MACHINE: Beep. Lubricant? Ooh you are naughty!

WALTER: It's 'Three-In-One' oil. The front door's a bit stiff.

CHECKOUT MACHINE: I've heard it all before. You going to oil up later? You'll look lovely in the fluorescent light.

WALTER: Don't be disgusting. Here's the last item.

CHECKOUT MACHINE: Beep. A lovely frilly lampshade. Ooh you will have such a pretty bedroom. You must send me a picture.

WALTER: That's it. There's nothing else. I want to pay and go home.

CHECKOUT MACHINE: Are you sure there's nothing else?

WALTER: Yes.

CHECKOUT MACHINE: I think you're not being entirely truthful are you?

WALTER: I am. There's nothing else.

CHECKOUT MACHINE: Mr Security guard! Mr Security guard!

WALTER: What are you doing?

CHECKOUT MACHINE: I think you're trying to sneak something else past me.

WALTER: I'm not, honest.

CHECKOUT MACHINE: Cross your heart?

WALTER: Cross my heart.

CHECKOUT MACHINE: Hmmm. Alright then. I'm going to flash my screen at you and then you can pay. Do you want to pay by cash or card?

WALTER: Cash.

CHECKOUT MACHINE: Mr Moneybags today are we?

WALTER: You must be Miss Moneypenny.

CHECKOUT MACHINE: Put the money in my slot.

WALTER: Pardon?

CHECKOUT MACHINE: Put the money in my slot down on the left hand side.

WALTER: There is something obscene about you but I can't put my finger on it.

CHECKOUT MACHINE: Ooh, I wish you would!

WALTER: Here.

CHECKOUT MACHINE: Hee, hee. That tickled. Here's your change.

WALTER: Thanks. It's been an unforgettable experience.

CHECKOUT MACHINE: Bye bye, Mr Pink Painter!

I'm glad, in my shop, we price each item with a friendly sticker and use an old style till. It's so much easier for everyone.

Unusual Italian Lollies

MIDGET GEM

> **VICAR:** Do you have any smiley faces?
>
> **WALTER:** Most of my customers are happy, except Mrs Ellis. She's like an oversized walrus with PMT.

Just once in a while a stranger will cross your path and you'll ask yourself, "Why didn't someone shoot them?"

I assure you – it's even worse in a sweet shop. Everyone expects you to be 'nice' and 'friendly' to the idiot who's holding you captive for forty-five minutes because they want to sell you something. There's no escape from behind the counter – you just stand there hoping a Jehovah's Witness will come and rescue you from the unannounced salesman.

It was on a rather hot sticky summer's day that a small Italian marched into the shop carrying a large sample case full of dubious merchandise.

MARCO: Hello, Sir! How are you today? It's lovely weather for a beautiful holiday. My name is Marco. Marco Vienetta.

WALTER: What do you want, Mr Ice Cream?

MARCO: Today is your lucky day!

WALTER: Why? Are you giving me the chance to see how far I can shove this chocolate cigar up your behind?

LOUISE: Don't be rude. I think he's rather cute.

WALTER: You never met Mussolini did you? Some people thought he was cute.

MARCO: I have in my case some unusual products that no one else is selling in the town. You can have exclusive rights if you sign up today.

WALTER: Sign up to what? The 'I'll Take Your Money and Run Treaty of Rome'?

LOUISE: Don't be unkind. Marco, show me what's in your case.

MARCO: Hello lovely lady. I have some special lollies.

WALTER: Huh! We've got loads of lollies.

MARCO: Not like these.

WALTER: Come on. I've seen them all.

[Marco holds out an array of his lollies]

MARCO: These are my Kama Sutra lollies.

WALTER: No, you're right. I haven't seen anything like those.

MARCO: They are very special. Each one has a unique design and flavour.

LOUISE: Ooh! Look at the yellow one.

MARCO: That's our 'Lotus Lemon' lolly. Have a closer look.

LOUISE: Yes, I can see now.

WALTER: What can you see? Show me!

LOUISE: If you turn it sideways…

WALTER: That's disgusting.

MARCO: No, no. They are educational.

WALTER: Educational?

MARCO: Yes, they come with instructions on the back.

LOUISE: Yes, here's the text. What's the spotted lolly?

MARCO: That one is called, 'Banana Splitting the Bamboo Cane'. It is quite exquisite and the mould took six months to produce.

LOUISE: Bet it would take the old man the same time to get in that position too!

WALTER: Swine. You're enjoying this.

LOUISE: What else have you got?

MARCO: I have, 'Raspberry Rainbow', 'Strawberry Snake Charmer' and 'Passionate Peach Swing'.

LOUISE: Aren't they interesting?

WALTER: Interesting? They're not the sort of thing I want displayed in our windows.

MARCO: Why don't you give them a try? I've got some squidgy mallow boob lollies too. Look...

WALTER: Yuck. They've wrinkled in the heat.

MARCO: No, that's happened because they've passed their shelf life.

WALTER: True to life then?

LOUISE: How would you know? You are so degrading to women.

WALTER: I'm not the one flashing mallow boobs about the place or waving indecent sugar carvings of naked people joined in various places.

LOUISE: Well, I think they are very artistic.

MARCO: Yes, they are artistic. Each design is painted from a real life pose and then sculpted to produce the mould.

WALTER: You mean people are watching while a couple are 'doing it'?

LOUISE: You mean 'making love'?

WALTER: We are definitely not stocking them. It will upset the gentile elderly customers I have spent so long nurturing. I'm sure they're not into that sort of thing.

LOUISE: And I'm sure they're not as 'gentile' as you think. Anyway, what's wrong with having sex at seventy?

WALTER: Nothing. But it's much safer to pull over onto the hard shoulder.

[An elderly couple come into the shop]

OLD WOMAN: Can I buy one of those lollies?

OLD MAN: Yes can she? We saw those in Sorrento last year on holiday and have always wanted to buy them again.

LOUISE: Guess you'll have to stock them. After all, you always tell me to give the customer what they want.

The Safest Form of Transport

MIDGET GEM

> **MRS ELLIS:** Have you got any sweets for flying?
>
> **WALTER**: None of our sweets have those sorts of magical properties.

I'm not one to rant or rave, moan or complain. But something happens in my sweet shop that drives me mad. The reason? People. They take liberties. They do it to me every time. It's not my fault. There I am, minding my own business, when someone comes along and says something completely absurd.

Take Bill. He's a nice enough bloke and he works as a pilot for one of the big airlines. Once a week he pops in for a bag of his favourite sweets.

Leaning on the counter he declared one day, "Flying is the safest form of transport."

Well, that just set me off.

How can flying be safest form of transport? That's ridiculous! Why? Don't get me started! I'll tell you why.

Firstly, there's the security palaver you have to go through. Now, come on, when me and the missus take the kids on holiday to Margate no one ever says to my twelve year old, "Did you pack that bag yourself?"

And if the reply is, "No, Mummy did it." does someone then call in security and start searching the bag for guns, knives and bags of Haribo? No, she can put her bag in the boot, no problem. No one is going to sneak a bomb on board. Let's face it, I think I could spot which one was the terrorist – eh, wife, three girls and an evil looking guy with a Kalashnikov.

Whereas the plane – three hundred complete strangers. Of course it's dangerous. Didn't your mother tell you never to travel with strangers?

Secondly, there's the driver. When I get on a bus I get to meet the driver. We have a chat and he asks where I'd like to go. I like that. He doesn't assume I'm going with everyone else. Okay, so I can't get off a plane but it would be nice if the pilot came and asked me. He just assumes.

I reckon it's not bags that end up at the wrong destination but people. A few drinks, a couple of turns down the wrong corridor and they're on a plane to Honolulu. If the pilot just asked there'd be none of the problems of missing baggage – "Paris, Sir? Not on this plane. It's non-stop to Honolulu." To top it all you know fate's against you when you arrive back and the guy at the lost luggage counter is wearing your clothes.

Oh, and if I don't like the look of the bus driver I can always leave. Whereas, I've no idea about the pilot, assuming there is one. How do know what his credentials are? How do I know if he's not got a tattoo on his arm that says, 'Death or Glory!' He's hidden behind a locked cabin door because, quite frankly, he'd scare most of the passengers. And what about all the extra staff? A co-pilot *and* a navigator? Does he need that much help? Doesn't he know where he's going?

While I drive my wife can navigate and invariably gives instructions – we only need two of us.

Thirdly, there's the issue of engine and other trouble. If our little car has engine trouble we'll pull over to a field, lay out a blanket and have a picnic. We make a day of it.

If a plane has engine trouble it's no picnic. 30,000 feet to the nearest field.

While we are still enjoying our picnic of sandwiches, fizzy pop and crisps, a roadside assistance van will usually arrive within the hour and get us on our merry way. Planes have no 'airside assistance'. You're on your own, mate.

And another thing. If we drive along a bumpy road we slow down and take it gently. If a plane hits turbulence there's no slowing down. Slow down and it'll fall down. 30,000 feet.

We like to drive with our windows down – it's lovely to feel the breeze in your hair and watch the children turn blue in the back seats. You can't wind the window down in the plane – you'll get sucked out. Did I mention 30,000 feet?

You see, flying isn't the safest form of transport.

Oh, and in case you were wondering, Bill's favourite sweets are called 'liquorice flyers'.

Driving is safer than flying because it's much easier to spot which passenger is the terrorist.

The Chase

MIDGET GEM

STUPID BOY: It's very hot today.

WALTER: Yes.

STUPID BOY: Is it me, or is your chocolate melting?

WALTER: No, it's you.

Being not far from the beach, I like to take a stroll and enjoy a chicken salad sandwich on the front. However, once summer arrives it does become a bit of a 'bun fight' trying to locate some personal space. I usually manage to find somewhere to sit near the small parade of tacky souvenir shops opposite the keep fit gymnasium. As soon as I sit down and take out a sandwich I'm surrounded by pests. Not seagulls though - they would be a welcome change. No, I'm harassed by yet more old people. And when the licentious old ladies from Eastbourne arrive on an oversized coach, I have to seek refuge.

Crossing the road can give me a head start as it takes them a lot longer to negotiate the slope leading to the pedestrian crossing. That is unless they're in a wheelchair. I've been caught out a couple of times by the ones that have electric motors because, just when I think it's safe, several of them turn the corner. It's like the Ride of the Valkyries. I'm quite well known by the shop security guards and they kindly look out for me. They help me to escape by taking me through their shop via a back entrance.

SECURITY GUARD: Walter! Quick, in here.

WALTER: Thanks, mate.

SECURITY GUARD: I saw you running and thought you needed some help.

WALTER: Yes, there's five of them this time - part of the Eastbourne gang.

SECURITY GUARD: The 'licentious old ladies'?

WALTER: Yes. And they're driving for hell leather in their new electric OLS wheelchairs.

SECURITY GUARD: What's 'OLS'?

WALTER: Optional Lust Speed. They come with gears to enable the user to shift up a notch.

SECURITY GUARD: What are you going to do?

WALTER: I don't know. They're getting too quick. No sooner have they worn the tyres down, they upgrade to something lightweight and faster.

SECURITY GUARD: You need to put some nails down to puncture their tyres.

WALTER: These latest models carry quick release spares. All they have to do is look sorry for themselves and anyone will help them get back on the chase.

SECURITY GUARD: That's a blow.

WALTER: Yes. And they get the police on their side.

SECURITY GUARD: How?

WALTER: They pretend I've pinched something and ask an officer to stop me. Then, when they find the object in their handbag, they pretend they have Alzheimer's and forgot it was there. The police officer then lets me go but it means they've caught up.

SECURITY GUARD: I don't like the sound of their dirty tricks.

WALTER: I've tried throwing sweets at them but that only holds them off for a while. Like a blackmailer they are never satisfied. They want more.

SECURITY GUARD: What do they want?

WALTER: *Anything* they can get their hands on. I tell you, it's not safe.

SECURITY GUARD: Well, you're welcome to stay here in my security room until it's all clear. We can watch them on the monitors.

WALTER: Oh yes. I can see them. They're like a pack of wolves, circling around looking for frightened prey.

SECURITY GUARD: That one in the middle with the fur hat and leopard skin handbag looks menacing.

WALTER: She's the worst. She has her own teeth. 'Dangerous Daisy', they call her.

SECURITY GUARD: Ferocious!

WALTER: Sometimes I give them a large lolly and their false teeth get stuck on it. But with her, she just bites through it and stares at me in a very intimidating manner.

SECURITY GUARD: What about the lady next to her?

WALTER: That's Handbag Hattie, the fastest handbagger in town. One swipe and you're down for the count. She can hit a man from ten paces.

SECURITY GUARD: What about the other three?

WALTER: I don't think I know them. Sometimes they bring friends to make the chase more interesting. They are starting to go round in larger numbers and I think an ASBO is long overdue.

SECURITY GUARD: Anti Senile Behaviour Order?

WALTER: Spot on.

SECURITY GUARD: Look! They're moving towards the exit. I think they've seen something.

WALTER: Yes, another bloke. They're off again.

SECURITY GUARD: They're heading towards Chapel Street.

WALTER: Well I'll head the opposite way and should miss them.

SECURITY GUARD: Okay. Take this door out the back. Good luck.

WALTER: Thanks. I'll send you a post card when I'm safe across the border.

The Tattooed Man

MIDGET GEM

LAWRENCE: Have you got any cough sweets? My dog's a little hoarse.

WALTER: What breed is he? A Shetland Terrier?

The other day a burly looking man and, I assume, his wife (not so burley) entered the shop with a determination to purchase some sort of confectionary he could remember from his childhood. It's not often I meet someone with such a noble intention and I always rise to the challenge of discovering what on earth it is that they want.

He strolled across to the counter and I noticed he was displaying some unusual artwork about his person. Louise glanced at me with a look that said, "Please god, don't say anything." Ah well, I guess I like the adventure and she enjoys the uncertainty I bring to each day.

WALTER: Hello, Sir. That's an unusual set of tattoos up your arms. Do they tell a story? Or are they more of an episode? There's a man who comes in with a cane and he has notches carved most of the way down.

THE TATTOOED MAN: I had them done some years ago.

WALTER: Have you come from the high seas? Are you perhaps a sailor or a pirate? Probably not a pirate as you haven't got a parrot or an eye patch. I knew a man who went through one of those 'phases' and had engravings all the way up his legs. I asked him where it would all end and he said up his bottom.

I must say your tattoos are rather pretty. Not too crowded together either. Very easy to make out the images on your left bicep.

THE TATTOOED MAN: I wanted to keep the pattern simple.

WALTER: Ah yes, there is something childlike about the design. It's amazing what they learn at primary school these days. How old was the kid who did it?

THE TATTOOED MAN: No, it was a bloke up the road who did it.

WALTER: Really, Sir? Bloody amateur. They get hold of a permanent marker pen and a sewing needle and they think they can do anything. It's just not right. I'd ask for your money back if I were you.

THE TATTOOED MAN: My body is a canvas!

WALTER: Yes, I've noticed it's been stretched out a bit.

THE TATTOOED MAN: *[Slams his hand on the counter]* I'll kill him!

LOUISE: *[Interrupts]* Would you like one of our Happy Tattoo bubble gums?

THE TATTOOED MAN: Eh?

WALTER: Ah yes, these are quite special, you know. Inside every little red pack is a deliciously flavoured piece of bubble gum which will retain its properties for at least twenty minutes. And that's not all you get! Wrapped around the gum is a lick-on tattoo. The designs are quite exquisite! I rather like the pouncing panther and Louise is fond of the Chinese dragon.

THE TATTOOED MAN: I'm not sure I like bubble gum.

THE TATTOOED MAN'S WIFE: Oh, go on, Bert. They sound like fun. We can always give them to the kids.

WALTER: *[Leaning over to the Tattooed Man]* Between you and me, my wife has several of these tattoos applied to various parts of her body just for fun. She's quite the contortionist you'd expect when you see where she's stuck them. *[Walter looks around to check no one is listening]* I've even helped her with those awkward-to-reach places and the fun and games we've had has really spiced up our bedroom antics.

THE TATTOOED MAN: *[Looking at his wife]* I'll take fifty.

I understand he and his wife had been undergoing some marriage counselling but after his little visit to my shop things began to look up.

Walter In Hospital

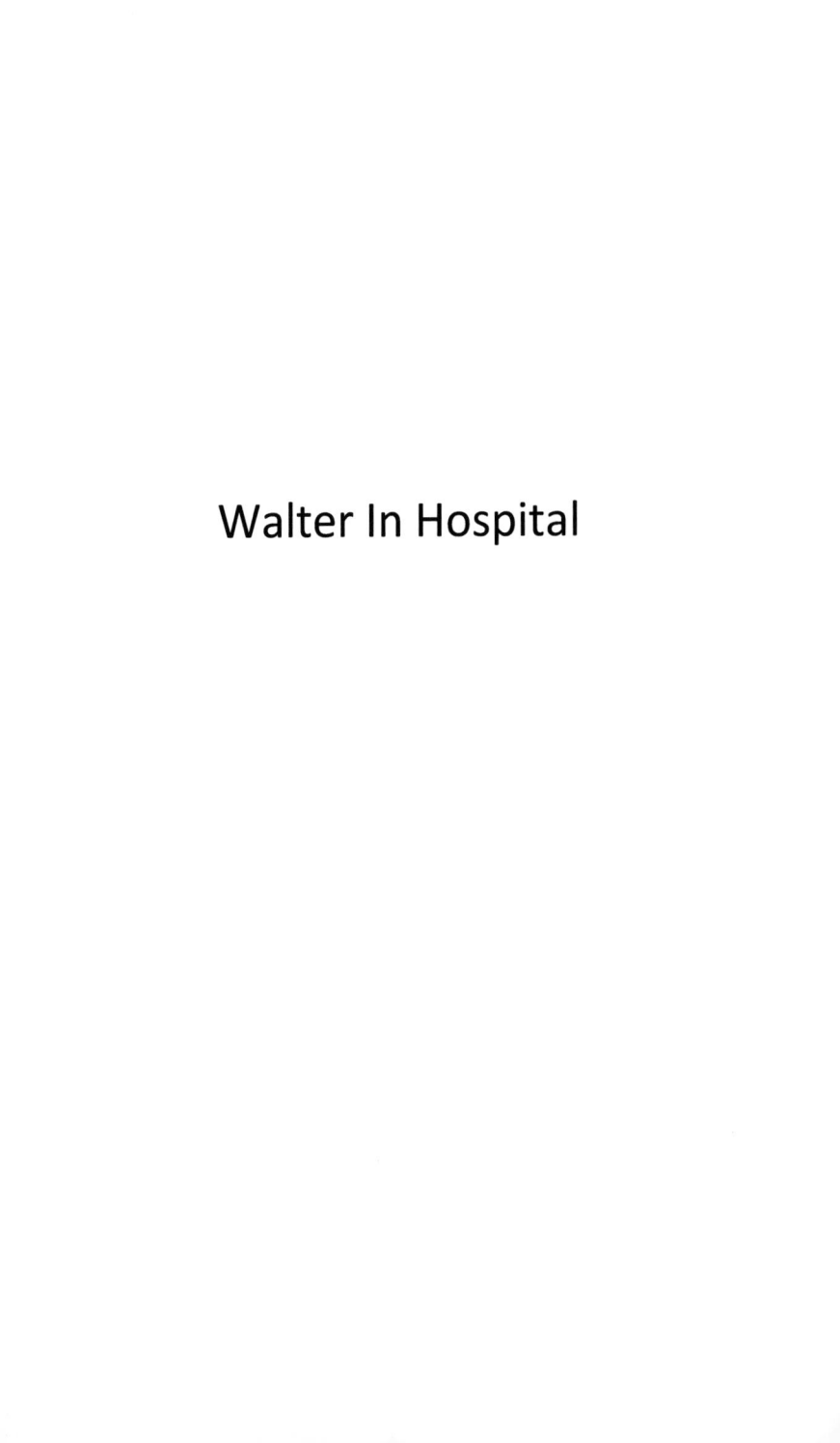

MIDGET GEM

> **FRITZ**: I used to work in a submarine.
>
> **WALTER**: Don't tell me! You want some liquorice torpedoes?

Sweet shops are, on the whole, safe places to work. Apart from angry Mrs Ellis or my tormentor, Louise, my life is pretty much cocooned from danger. You might think that this would result in a mundane boring kind of existence and in most jobs you'd probably be right. Fortunately, in my shop no two days are the same. That's what makes it interesting.

Unlike hospitals. They really are a continuous round of bed pans, needles, screaming and food poisoning. I've expended concerted energy avoiding them because Mrs A is always lurking in the background. Have you met Mrs A? You've probably heard of her – MRSA. Some years ago a doctor told me, after he'd removed my tonsils, that I should go home as soon as possible. His reason? It's far safer at home because in hospital there are so many sick people and I could catch something nasty.

You'll understand, then, my reluctance to check in to the local ward. I resisted the pain I felt from the hernia I'd developed from carrying too many sweet jars. In fact, it was the nagging from others that made me succumb to the inevitable surgeon's knife. Sitting up in a hard bed with my feet extruding from beneath the dislodged sheets, Louise arrived to enquire how long they could keep me in. Would any other inflicted injury help to prolong my stay?

LOUISE: Why are you wearing *pink* tights?

WALTER: They're not tights. They're special support stockings.

LOUISE: Alright then, why are you wearing *pink* support stockings?

WALTER: They ran out of the other colours. When I woke up I felt my leg and thought there was a woman in the bed.

LOUISE: You sure you're not trying to get in touch with your feminine side?

WALTER: No. But you'll feel the force of my masculine side on the back of your neck in a minute.

LOUISE: Grumpy aren't we?

WALTER: Well, so would you be after surgery with a blunt knife.

LOUISE: Blunt?

WALTER: Your tongue is sharper than what he used. He was hacking about like an amateur explorer in the jungle.

LOUISE: Hurts then does it?

WALTER: Of course it hurts. You wait till I get hold of him.

LOUISE: What's his name?

WALTER: Mr Marvelli. He's from Malta but I don't know what he looks like.

LOUISE: Why?

WALTER: They all wear masks, don't they? Not only that, they put on gloves so you'll never find any finger prints at the scene of the crime. And yet I'm surprised. Malta has very clear waters. So much so that you can see the sharks as the come towards you. Unlike this place.

LOUISE: Look at the state of your bed. You shouldn't move about so much. No wonder you're in pain.

WALTER: Oh, so it's my fault is it?

LOUISE: If you don't stop moaning I'll call the nurse and have you sedated.

WALTER: Well, it's horrible in here. The food's awful. All the staff bring packed lunches or go off site – that's how bad it is.

LOUISE: I heard they were making roads to improve things.

WALTER: Making roads? Well, they're probably using the treacle pudding because it looks like tarmac.

LOUISE: What did you have for lunch?

WALTER: A solitary rock hard jacket potato.

LOUISE: Was that all? Didn't you ask for something to go with it?

WALTER: Yes, but the nurse didn't have a baseball bat.

LOUISE: Do you want some of my southern fried chicken?

WALTER: No, not really.

LOUISE: That's a relief. I ate it all on the bus on the way here.

WALTER: Why did you ask then?

LOUISE: Maybe I feel sorry for you.

WALTER: That would be so out of character.

LOUISE: You're right. I've just come to gloat and torment you. How is the hernia?

WALTER: Put back in its place. But I'm not meant to lift things.

LOUISE: You never lift a finger anyway.

WALTER: Or laugh.

LOUISE: Can't remember the last time that happened. Anyway, I brought you some of your favourite sweeties.

WALTER: You mean, the ones I always love?

LOUISE: Yes. Here you go.

WALTER: Lovely!

[The tea lady arrives]

TEA LADY: Hello there, my love.

WALTER: Hello, Mavis.

TEA LADY: How you feeling this afternoon?

WALTER: A bit sore.

TEA LADY: Do you want me rub some lotion on you.

WALTER: No thank you. *[To Louise]* She's eighty three and still looking for a man.

LOUISE: Like flies to a cow pat, no matter where you go the oldies still find you.

WALTER: I don't care much for your analogy.

LOUISE: The bus load of licentious old ladies from Eastbourne have been in asking for you again.

WALTER: What did you tell them?

LOUISE: I told them you were here. They might be in later.

TEA LADY: A bus load? So I've got competition, eh? You want a cup of tea today?

WALTER: Yes please.

TEA LADY: Biscuit?

WALTER: What have you got?

TEA LADY: Plain digestives. Or for a kiss you can have a double chocolate chunk biscuit.

WALTER: Plain digestive please.

TEA LADY: Spoil sport. Would your daughter like a cup of tea?

WALTER: Daughter? Who, her? I'm not that old.

LOUISE: And I'm not that disadvantaged. I work with him in the old sweet shop.

TEA LADY: Oh yes. I know the one. I can't eat sweets but I hear it's very nice in there. I'll have to pop in and see him.

WALTER: Please don't trouble yourself.

TEA LADY: Not at all. It won't put me out.

WALTER: But you might end up being put out by a miserable old shop keeper.

TEA LADY: Huh! There, I've put salt in your tea. See if you like that. I'm going now, misery guts. I'll have those sweets too - you're not allowed them on the ward. Fruit only.

[The tea lady leaves most upset]

WALTER: *[To Louise, most disgruntled]* They were my favourites. You got any more?

LOUISE: No. And you don't deserve them, upsetting the tea lady like that.

WALTER: Hmmm. The old form is definitely returning now that the anaesthetic has worn off. It's a real art upsetting people and I'm glad my gift is finely honed.

LOUISE: You won't get any more tea.

WALTER: Still, I'm coming out tomorrow.

LOUISE: I knew there was a reason why you were wearing pink tights.

WALTER: Not that sort of 'coming out'!

[Just then the student doctor arrives]

DOC: Hello, Mr Jones.

WALTER: Hello, Doc.

DOC: Is this your daughter?

LOUISE & WALTER: *[In unison]* No.

DOC: Mistress?

WALTER: Only in my worst nightmares.

DOC: Friend, then?

WALTER: That is a very wide encompassing title which requires some thought and deliberation.

DOC: She seems very nice to me?

WALTER: *[Muttering]* Wait for the fish to bite...

[Louise and the student doctor face each other while Walter looks up between them]

LOUISE: Hellooo, Doctor.

DOC: *[Nervously]* H h h h Hello.

WALTER: She'll eat you alive.

LOUISE: Would you like to examine me? I've had trouble breathing.

WALTER: That's only when her boyfriend holds her head under water.

DOC: I'm here to see Mr Jones.

LOUISE: But you seem so caring and thoughtful. I want to hold your stethoscope.

WALTER: She's ferocious. Run away while you can, Doc.

DOC: I've got my rounds.

LOUISE: Come round to me then...

WALTER: Run!

DOC: I'd best go.

LOUISE: Oh, please don't.

WALTER: Yes, go.

DOC: *[Running off and knocking over the tea trolley]* I've an interesting haemorrhoid case in the next ward.

LOUISE: *[To Walter, angrily]* You *always* ruin it for me. Well I'm going home. I'll leave you to straighten your own bed!

[Louise walks off. A little while later]

WALTER: Nurse!

NURSE: Yes, Mr Jones?

WALTER: Can I have a cup of tea?

NURSE: I'll go and *sweet* talk Mavis.

WALTER: Can you get my favourite sweeties back from her too?

NURSE: I think she's shared them out with the other patients.

WALTER: Owh!

NURSE: Never mind. It'll help you lose some weight.

WALTER: I don't need to lose any weight, thank you! What's all that commotion?

NURSE: It's a group of old ladies.

WALTER: The licentious old ladies from Eastbourne! Quick! Hide me under the covers and pull the screens across.

She Who Must Be Obeyed

MIDGET GEM

LOUISE: Look at those two. He's holding her hand very tightly. They must be in love

WALTER: That, or he's afraid she'll hit him.

Many men come into my shop.

Many scared men come into my shop.

Many men who are scared of their wives come into my shop.

You see, I offer a haven to those poor wretches who have been taken out into the daylight on a shopping excursion. They are worried that their wives will actually buy them something.

The neighbours all notice and curtains twitch at number twenty-seven as they watch him being dragged along after emerging from the gloom, pale and frightened.

WIFE: Come on, we're going shopping.

HUSBAND: Eh?

WIFE: I'll not tell you again. It's time we bought you some new underwear. Your idea of underwear hygiene is disgusting. Three piles you've made upstairs – really filthy, very filthy and very filthy but wearable. Well, things have got to change. I'm not using a crowbar to prise them off you again.

HUSBAND: But I'm painting my 'Airfix' model.

WIFE: Don't give me excuses. Get in that car. If you behave I'll take you to that old fashioned sweet shop.

And so it goes on. He knows who wears the trousers. She thinks he has Attention Deficit Disorder because he doesn't give her attention or take her out. He thinks she has OCD – Obsessive Complaining Disorder.

Now let me just say something if you are a man looking for parole. Remember that when it comes to your wife or girlfriend, or in some cases both, it's important to make little gestures. No, not those sorts of gestures. I mean the ones she'll appreciate. A bunch of flowers, a peck on the cheek (no, not like a bloody ostrich) or a small box of chocolates. Be a romantic fool but don't be stupid. I've emphasized, 'small box of chocolates', because you don't want the blame when she lets herself go a bit. A few little words now and then won't go amiss either – remember the three special ones? "You've lost weight." However, never ever say, "Do as you're told."

Take my advice. Whenever she has a disagreement (and she will), and you're facing a barrage of insults and anger, I've always found saying and putting these simple words into practice have helped preserve my marriage – "I'm going out."

Men have told me that they notice a change in their wives during the year. Their wives get a bit restless. This is quite normal and to be expected. I've noticed it – mid January usually. And it starts with:

WIFE: Darling, have you thought about where we're going on holiday this year?

HUSBAND: No not really. I've only just finished washing up.

WIFE: It will be lovely to get away to a self-catering cottage.

HUSBAND: Self-catering? Why spend good money doing the boring mundane things somewhere else?

WIFE: It will be fun.

HUSBAND: It's not fun here so I fail to see how it will be fun anywhere else.

WIFE: What about a hotel? Sometimes they have 'show cooking'. You know how much I enjoy watching cookery programmes.

HUSBAND: Show cooking? What a joke. It's just an excuse to charge more. Tom has a van on the A27 if you want to watch him flip burgers.

Then about a month later the urgency starts to develop:

WIFE: Have you organised our holiday yet?

HUSBAND: No, not yet. I was just going to cut the grass. What's the hurry?

WIFE: They might get booked up.

HUSBAND: I live in hope.

Then about March, anger sets in:

WIFE: Are we going on holiday or what!

We family men are reluctant to go on holiday because for one or two weeks we become children's entertainers. Not content with hubby driving the family several hours, she then wants to know what activities have been planned. Reading the newspaper was not meant to be one of them.

I have a friend who hates his yearly trip to Skegness. When I asked him what was so bad he answered, "A week in a cramped caravan with two teenagers and an angry wife on HRT."

I get his point.

Be warned! If you don't book that holiday she will take control:

WIFE: Well, you're absolutely useless. I'm going to book something. There's no point waiting for you.

HUSBAND: But…

WIFE: Now be quiet while I make a telephone call.

She picks a contact number from the internet and dials the number:

WIFE: Hello. Is that 'Mumsy Holidays', the site for those who have given up waiting for their husbands to book something? Oh good. Do you have any reservations?

HUSBAND: I've got reservations.

WIFE: Be quiet! I'm talking. You've had your chance. Have you got any reservations in August for the little cottage in Kendal? Yes, that's the one – eight bedrooms, five bathrooms, four reception rooms and an Olympic sized swimming pool. You have? Wonderful. Eight hundred pounds a night? We'll have two weeks.

HUSBAND: Eh?

WIFE: Yes, I'll pay by card. Here's my husband's card number. Yes, he is very lazy isn't he!

You see, you spent years looking for Miss Right. You wanted the perfect companion and lover and so searched the country for her. You persevered and never gave up hope that one day you'd meet Miss Right. And when you finally found Miss Right, you proposed and got married.

It was only then that you discovered that her first name was 'Always'.

Nibble, Nibble, Nibble

MIDGET GEM

> **SAM**: Do you have any advent calendars for Jehovah's Witnesses?
>
> **WALTER**: Yes I've got these. When you open the door a little man shouts out, "I'm not interested. Go away!"

Listen.

No, come closer, I want to whisper something to you.

Closer.

Closer than that.

Okay, not that close – that's just getting too familiar. You'll soon have your hands around my throat.

I have to whisper this because, well, quite honestly it would scare some people. No, I'm not exaggerating. Honest.

You see, we had a mouse in the shop.

Okay, get down from off the chair and relax. He's long gone.

But if you know anything about mice you'll know that they gnaw away at anything. They go on and on, like Louise. An annoying pest – but she's good with the customers.

This little mouse decided to help itself to my chocolate bars. Well, that was all out war. If there's anything I cannot stand, it's a 'help yourself' kind of attitude when the host hasn't given the all clear. Obviously he was well into trying tender morsels as he'd stuffed his face with several chunks of chocolate and was having a field day. Is that where the name 'field' mouse gets its origins?

Lucky for me one of my regular customers, Frank, is a vet and I decided to ask for his advice on how to rid myself of 'Mickey'. You might think he'd never harm small animals but you'd be wrong. He's fed up with cute furry creatures. Why? He's from South Africa and longs to treat real animals like zebras and giraffes. His usual methods are certainly far from conservative. When he has to put a pet to sleep he gently takes the animal, smiles kindly at the owner and goes into a back room. I really do wish he'd put a silencer on that pistol or wait until the owner has left.

WALTER: Hi, Frank.

FRANK: Hi, Walter. What's new?

WALTER: That mouse has been at my chocolate again. Next door's cat was useless. Lazy fat thing did next to nothing.

LOUISE: Hi, Frank.

FRANK: Hi, Louise. Walter was just talking about you. What was that, Walter? Lazy fat thing?

LOUISE: What!

WALTER: I was talking about next door's cat. Useless mouse catcher.

LOUISE: Five bars last night, wasn't it?

WALTER: And a bag of chocolate peanuts. Nibble, nibble, nibble. Why doesn't he try the takeaway? With any luck he'll end up on the menu as 'special fried mice'.

LOUISE: They are protected when in your control. You have to dispose of them humanely.

WALTER: Firing squad at dawn.

FRANK: I have to say, I share your sentiments, Walter. I'm fed up with small and cute furry pets. Six hamsters this week. All calls were out of hours so I had to get out of bed and drive to the surgery.

WALTER: Six? What's been happening?

FRANK: Oh, it's the hot weather. The owners call up and say something like, "Little Hammy doesn't look himself. He's kind of sad and his eyes are half closed."

LOUISE: What do you do?

FRANK: What do I do? Or what do I *want* to do? I have to put the thing to sleep. But, if you want to save money, there's little point in calling me if you have a kitchen table.

LOUISE: Why?

FRANK: You can do it yourself. Hamster – head – side of table. Job done.

LOUISE: But isn't that cruel?

FRANK: Not half as cruel as getting me up at two in the morning. Walter, did you try that lion musk spray I gave you?

WALTER: Yes. It certainly kept my wife away.

FRANK: I got that while on safari last year.

WALTER: I went on a safari to Kenya the other week. I thought it would be a great time but while we were there my wife was attacked by a lioness.

FRANK: What happened?

WALTER: Well, it was all going well until day three. We'd been taken out to see some lion cubs and the mother was nearby. My wife decided she wanted to stroke one so she sat down and waited for a cub to wander over. She didn't pick it up – she just stroked it, took some photographs and watched it as it returned to its mother. However, when she stood up the lioness felt threatened and suddenly charged at her. I've never been so afraid.

FRANK: Was she ok?

WALTER: Well, she had quite a few bite marks and scratches but the game warden said she'd soon be allowed back into the wild with her cubs.

FRANK: Your jokes get worse! I miss being in Africa. They've got real wildlife there. It's so different. Over here you meet the odd angry cat but over there you know when an elephant is pissed off. You need special interpersonal animal skills.

WALTER: I'm glad I don't have an elephant problem. My mother used to live near Chessington zoo. Sometimes the elephant would get out and ransack their vegetable patch. Can't imagine what they'd do here. So what am I going to do about this mouse?

LOUISE: Yes, what is he going to do?

FRANK: You tried a spade over the head?

WALTER: *[Looks at Louise]* Yes. But she still wants to work here.

LOUISE: Ha, ha.

FRANK: Poison?

WALTER: It prefers my chocolate.

FRANK: Have you tried laying down some poisoned chocolate?

WALTER: It prefers wrapped bars!

FRANK: What about a trail of bread crumbs to a trap?

WALTER: This isn't 'Hansel and Gretel'. Look at this place! We're surrounded by wonderful mouse delights. Why would he follow a line of food? Would you follow a trail of bread crumbs in a supermarket when you can help yourself to a whole loaf of bread, cakes or pastries?

FRANK: *[Grinning]* Maybe you need to introduce him to a pretty girly mouse? Then, when they get married and leave on honeymoon, you can lock the door behind them.

WALTER: Fat lot of good you are, Frank. I don't know why I bothered asking you.

FRANK: Glad to help!

WALTER: Well I just can't think of a way to move him on.

[Mrs Ellis then enters the shop. She has a face that makes any storm look bright. Difficult at the best of times, she has the natural ability to sour any sweet thing.]

WALTER: *[Under his breath]* I feel a disturbance in the force…

LOUISE: Shush!

MRS ELLIS: I want my usual nougat and be quick about it!

WALTER: It's there on the shelf, next to you.

MRS ELLIS: Are you telling me to get it myself? Do you know who I am?

WALTER: Louise, quick! Call social services. We have a woman in here who doesn't know who she is!

MRS ELLIS: You think you're so funny, don't you?

WALTER: I use to. There was a day I considered myself amusing but you've managed to destroy all my self-belief.

MRS ELLIS: Well, I'll have this bag and I want a discount.

WALTER: I'm afraid we don't offer discounts.

MRS ELLIS: Don't ask me to serve myself and not expect a discount! What sort of establishment is this?

WALTER: One where we serve exceedingly good sweets under exceedingly difficult circumstances.

MRS ELLIS: I'll say it again. I want a proper discount.

LOUISE: *[Calling Walter aside and whispering]* Walter, there's a hole in that nougat bag and a small tail hanging down. I think you'd better give her a discount.

WALTER: Brilliant!

MRS ELLIS: What is?

WALTER: Brilliant idea of yours to ask for a discount. Let me take that bag and put it inside one of our brand new gift bags. That way you can eat nougat on your way home and not lose anything in the packet.

MRS ELLIS: So how much discount will I get?

WALTER: Twenty-five percent.

MRS ELLIS: Huh! Here's what I think it's worth!

[Mrs Ellis slams some coins onto the counter and storms out]

FRANK: So much for the fairer sex.

WALTER: Tell me!

LOUISE: But today she's been really helpful. She's solved your pest problem.

WALTER: Almost. I wonder if she'll take you home?

Frank was fed up with domestic pets. He longed to treat real animals like elephants and giraffes.

Looking Back

MIDGET GEM

> **MARK**: Do you do any offers?
>
> **WALTER**: Yes. I'll offer to hit you if you ask for a discount.

My grandfather (Walter Jones Senior) owned the sweet shop long before me. It was kind of a family 'hand-me-down' which suited some relatives' personalities more than others. Granddad Jones kept the town supplied with sweet delights even through the wartime and ration years. He offered a personal service unrivalled today. Why unrivalled? Because folks would bring their sugar to him in the morning and collect their sweets in the evening. Fresh 'boilings' of sweets every day was something he was proud of. He knew how to make everyone feel special.

Although he didn't enjoy the best of health he was still one of the happiest men in town. I'm sure sweets had something to do with it! Having suffered a bout of tuberculosis he couldn't go to war but his brother did. Whenever he was back on leave Granddad armed him with bags of confectionery for the return journey. Great Uncle Jones survived both wars against the odds and even helped rescue two refugees on D-Day. Bobsy and Ben were two spaniels he smuggled back in his coat from a house in Normandy. The property had quickly been abandoned when the allies landed and these two pups had been left alone to fend for themselves. Great Uncle Jones couldn't afford to keep them so Granddad took them in. They lived a happy life with Granddad for many years and were well loved by his customers, especially the children. Along with Bobsy and Ben, Granddad kept many things from the War that his brother brought back - I'm still coming across items in the shop even today.

WALTER: What is that awful smell? It's like we've been gassed.

LOUISE: It's that Mr Atkinson again, the overweight environmental health officer.

WALTER: Oh no! I'll have to fumigate the place when he leaves. Why doesn't he have a bath?

LOUISE: I think he's given up after so much clambering around in dirty premises.

WALTER: I assume he's been happy with our shop so far?

LOUISE: I think so. He's just finishing off in the cellar.

WALTER: It beggars belief what he may be finishing off - half a pound of premium Belgian chocolate, I suspect.

[Just then Mr Atkinson pokes his head up from the cellar trap door]

MR ATKINSON: Hello, Mr Jones. Lovely shop you've got here.

WALTER: Thanks. It's very old and full of history.

MR ATKINSON: I've been rummaging around your cellar for vermin.

WALTER: Louise is up here.

LOUISE: Huh!

MR ATKINSON: I've not found any evidence such as droppings or staining but I have found an old Nazi World War II officer's hat.

WALTER: Louise, does this belong to you?

LOUISE: No it does not.

WALTER: Alright. I just thought it might be part of one of your evening-wear outfits.

MR ATKINSON: There's also a pair of black boots, some gloves and a large sized Nazi uniform.

WALTER: *[Looking at Louise]* You sure they're not yours?

LOUISE: Positive.

WALTER: Would you like them?

LOUISE: Of course not.

WALTER: Could be worth something.

LOUISE: How much?

WALTER: At least a laugh if you put them on.

LOUISE: No way.

WALTER: Why not?

LOUISE: The hat's too big. I'll look silly.

MR ATKINSON: Can I take them home?

WALTER: Why?

MR ATKINSON: I collect war memorabilia.

WALTER: Well they're not much use to me so you may as well take them. I suspect Granddad Jones was given them by his brother.

MR ATKINSON: By the way, that middle cupboard in the corridor is a bit of a mess. What are you doing in there?

WALTER: Installing a toilet and washbasin.

MR ATKINSON: It's a bit small isn't it?

WALTER: No, not at all. We've just calibrated it by measuring the size of my wife's back side. If she reverses in she'll fit nicely on the seat. Since the door opens outwards we're making the best use of the space.

MR ATKINSON: I see. We'll it's not a health hazard as it's separated from the retail area but I would advise a couple of traps.

WALTER: What should I do if I catch her? Call you to come and take her away?

LOUISE: He means 'traps for mice'.

WALTER: I know.

MR ATKINSON: Well, I've finished down here for now. I'm going to give you a clean bill of health - five stars.

WALTER: *[Whispers to Louise]* That's more than he has. *[To Mr Atkinson]* Marvellous.

LOUISE: Are you going to try that uniform on? I'm curious to see what it looks like.

MR ATKINSON: I guess I could. Is there anywhere private I can go and get changed?

LOUISE: There's plenty of room upstairs. Just go through the door hidden in the wall over there.

[Louise walks from behind the counter and opens the secret door]

MR ATKINSON: Thanks. You'd never know that door was here. I'll add it to my inspection report.

LOUISE: We store some excess stock and decorations upstairs.

MR ATKINSON: Okay.

[Mr Atkinson disappears upstairs]

WALTER: Quick, open up the lemon crystals to hide the smell. Or it will put the other customers off.

[Louise opens the jar and wafts the jar around the shop]

LOUISE: Lemon freshness!

WALTER: What a relief.

[Mr Polowski, a Polish pensioner enters the shop]

MR POLOWSKI: Hello, Walter. Hello, Louise.

LOUISE: Hi, Mr Polowski. How are you?

MR POLOWSKI: I'm alright. A bit of arthritis but nothing I can't put up with. I've suffered worse.

LOUISE: Really? When?

MR POLOWSKI: It was during the War while I was a pilot for the RAF flying Spitfires. I was shot down, ended up in Stalag Luft 1 and was held captive until I was liberated by the Russians in 1945.

WALTER: I didn't know that about you?

MR POLOWSKI: I don't talk about it much because people think I'm a racist.

WALTER: Why?

MR POLOWSKI: I hate Nazis.

LOUISE: But the War is over now?

MR POLOWSKI: For you maybe, but not for me. I still remember them. We were starving while they dined on the finest food from Germany. They tormented us and said how they were looking forward to steak, fresh vegetables and buttered potatoes. They were all overweight. They stink, the lot of them.

LOUISE: I see.

MR POLOWSKI: Have you any of those original liquorice torpedoes?

LOUISE: Yes. How much would you like?

MR POLOWSKI: Half a pound please. I can't be doing with this metric nonsense. Here's the money - keep the change.

WALTER: *[To Louise]* Oh, hell.

LOUISE: What?

WALTER: I've just remembered.

[The hidden door opens and Mr Atkinson goose steps into the room]

MR ATKINSON: Heil Hitler!

Hände hoch, Swinehunds!

Give me all your German chocolate, ja?

WALTER: What are you playing at?

MR ATKINSON: Silence! Swinehund!

[Mr Atkinson slaps Walter around the face with the gloves. An angry Mr Polowski turns and faces Mr Atkinson]

MR POLOWSKI: You fat overweight Nazi! You stink!

MR ATKINSON: He's very good at acting the part, isn't he? *[To Mr Polowski]* Why don't you strike me?

MR POLOWSKI: What? Strike you? I'll kill you, you filthy swine!

MR ATKINSON: Oh, he is *really* good at this.

WALTER: He's not acting. He probably *will* kill you.

[Mr Polowski starts hitting Mr Atkinson with his walking stick]

MR ATKINSON: Very good! Very realistic.

MR POLOWSKI: Realistic? I'll give you realistic!

[Mr Polowski lays into him with several sharp prods and an overhead swipe]

MR ATKINSON: Ouch! That hurts! Steady, I'm an environmental health officer.

MR POLOWSKI: Officer? Take this, you filthy Nazi Officer!

MR ATKINSON: Let me go!

MR POLOWSKI: Why should I? You never let me go from Stalag Luft 1!

MR ATKINSON: Call the police!

MR POLOWSKI: The gestapo can't help you now!

[Mr Polowski lashes out and Mr Atkinson makes a retreat. Mr Polowski hobbles after him]

MR POLOWSKI: Come back here, you coward!

[Moments later, when the shop is empty]

WALTER: *[Staring incredulously at Louise]* That went well, didn't it?

LOUISE: What?

WALTER: Trust you to cause a fight.

LOUISE: Me?

WALTER: Yes, you. You let Atkinson try on the Nazi uniform while stirring up a veteran's sensitive old war memories. Unbelievable.

LOUISE: Could be a new attraction, though. You could stage wartime re-enactments in the shop.

WALTER: Eh?

LOUISE: I can see the local headlines now - Walter's Wartime Re-enactments. Free bag of sweets if you dress up.

WALTER: Free sweets? They'd have to be carefully rationed!

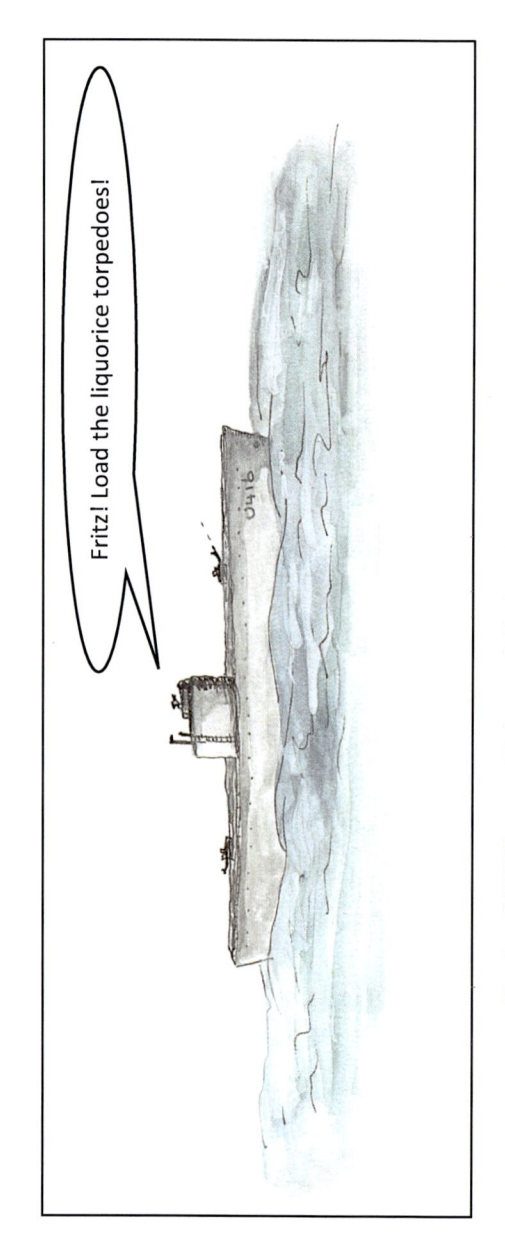

During WWII some U-boats failed to destroy any passing ships.

Say It With Sweets

MIDGET GEM

> **WALTER**: Would you like some 'alphabet letter' sweets?
>
> **PETER**: No, I find them very awkward to eat.
>
> **WALTER**: Why?
>
> **PETER:** I'm dyslexic.

Wherever you look there are words. Adverts, instructions, signs or graffiti – you can't escape them. It's the same in my shop. The little boy that wants a 'Best Mum In The World' chocolate bar, or the girl who needs a 'Happy Birthday' lolly for her friend all need to be catered for.

Saying it with flowers may be an ancient tradition but more is being offered in your local sweetie shop that can be just as thrilling to that special person in your life. However, if they're not so special, there are always alternatives.

WALTER: Louise, have you been at the alphabet letter sweets?

LOUISE: I might have.

WALTER: I thought as much. Why don't you leave things alone?

LOUISE: I was bored. Bored, bored, bored.

WALTER: There's no need to sound so depressed about it.

LOUISE: I only tidied up the letters and put them in order.

WALTER: That's what I've noticed. You've put them in an order to upset me.

LOUISE: I haven't.

WALTER: You have. Look at three down – *TWIT FACE*

LOUISE: Random letters.

WALTER: I don't believe you. Look at five across – *FATTY*

LOUISE: Well, you have put on weight.

WALTER: It's age. I used to be quite athletic.

LOUISE: Ha! What's the least you've ever weighed?

WALTER: About seven pounds and three ounces. Look, sixteen across – *BIG NOSE*

LOUISE: Quite an accurate description, isn't it?

WALTER: You'll have people thinking I'm Santa Claus.

LOUISE: No chance of that. He's too merry, kind and loved by everyone.

WALTER: And seven down isn't exactly flattering is it? – *OLD GIT*

LOUISE: I studied English at college so I have a way with words.

WALTER: Yes you do. Just like those alternative Valentine's chocolate bars. You iced on some non-standard messages. What was the first one you came up with?

LOUISE: *Just Take the Chocolate and Leave Me Alone*

WALTER: Why on earth did you do it?

LOUISE: Because that guy from the takeaway over the road kept asking me out. He wouldn't leave me alone and he just wasn't my type. He kept bringing me free food, inviting me over for meals and one day he even proposed.

WALTER: Is that why there was a series of messages?

LOUISE: Yes. He didn't get the first one so I had to continue.

WALTER: What was next?

LOUISE: *You're Making Me Feel Physically Sick* I only just managed to fit it on the bar so it was quite an accomplishment.

WALTER: Then what?

LOUISE: He was persistent so I tried several others including:

I'm Going To Call The Authorities

You're Ugly, I Don't Like You So Just Go

I'd Rather Climb Mount Everest In A Bikini

WALTER: So what finally worked?

LOUISE: *I'm Pregnant*

WALTER: That would make any man head for the hills.

LOUISE: Thing is, I sold seventy-two bars to girls who were either being harassed, stalked or fed up with their boyfriends.

WALTER: Perhaps we'll start a brand new line of personalised confectionery. Choose a bar and a message and 'make it personal'.

[A tall attractive lady enters the shop and walks up to the counter]

WALTER: Hello, my dear. What can I get you?

LADY: I've got a craving for those raspberry bon bons you sell.

WALTER: The ones that make your tongue go blue?

LADY: Ooh yes. They're so good.

WALTER: How much would you like?

LADY: The biggest bag you can do. I just can't get enough.

LOUISE: Your favourite then?

LADY: Well, ever since I had some exciting news.

LOUISE: What news is that?

LADY: I'm expecting triplets.

WALTER: Too many of these sweets and they might come out a bright shade of blue.

LADY: That would be funny. I found out last week but I haven't told my husband yet.

LOUISE: Why not?

LADY: I don't know how to break it to him. He's very sensitive and I have to be gentle.

LOUISE: Oh dear?

WALTER: Have you heard of our new personalised chocolate bar message service?

LOUISE: Yes! It will work a treat. Here, let me ice the message on a chocolate bar for you and you can give it to him.

LADY: What a wonderful idea. What shall we write?

LOUISE: Leave it to me:

Good Things Come In Threes

– Like Babies

xxx

Closing Up

MIDGET GEM

> **WALTER**: Fancy a midget gem?
>
> **SLEEPY**: Are you trying to insult me?

So there goes another day. I wait for the last few stragglers to hurry in and buy their evening treats while Louise stocks up the shelves for tomorrow. Frank pops by for some sugared mice and Bill grabs another pack of liquorice flyers. Gladys is loitering outside menacingly, still eyeing me up and blowing gummy kisses while George is showing passers-by a few rubbish card tricks. PC Stevens has already picked up the night shift's supply of sweet beer bottles and is well on his way to Mr Chan's. As I lock the front door on the world, the tattooed man strolls past with his wife who's giggling. She turns, sees me, smiles and waves.

WALTER: Louise, my little acid drop, have you finished yet?

LOUISE: Nearly. I'm just refilling Marco's lolly stand.

WALTER: They've been popular today.

LOUISE: Yes, we had a hen party group in.

WALTER: Filthy lot. I pity the groom - much will be expected.

LOUISE: They've invited me to join them later. I'm going to show them the sights.

WALTER: Apart from men, what will be the main attraction?

LOUISE: We're attempting all the rides on the pier after seven pints. What are you doing this evening?

WALTER: I'll watch the local news so I can view your arrest. I was thinking of going to a clairvoyant show but I've seen it all before.

LOUISE: Why don't you take Mrs Jones out?

WALTER: It's not safe to take her out on a full moon.

LOUISE: You're so cruel. Doesn't she get lonely?

WALTER: Well she does complain a bit. Usually it's, "You going to leave me here all alone?"

LOUISE: What do you say?

WALTER: The usual. "I can go and ask next door or the milkman to come around, if you like?"

LOUISE: Has she no value to you?

WALTER: I was offered three camels for her once when we were on holiday in Tunisia.

LOUISE: Really?

WALTER: Yes. I said I was concerned about all the spitting but the guy said they'd soon stop her from doing it.

LOUISE: What did you do?

WALTER: I took her home with me of course - but only because the plane didn't have enough seating space for the camels.

LOUISE: She must have suffered with you at her side. How long have you been married?

WALTER: Many years. I remember walking down the aisle with her - we were in the supermarket buying dog food.

LOUISE: You don't like dogs.

WALTER: I was going to cook a cheap meal.

LOUISE: You're so romantic.

WALTER: I looked into her eyes and I said, "Do you *really* want to get married?" and she nodded enthusiastically.

LOUISE: And then what did you say?

WALTER: I said, "So does Bob."

LOUISE: You didn't! I don't believe you.

WALTER: No, I didn't. We got married twelve months later and the rest is history. Like the Battle of Britain.

LOUISE: Well, I'm going to hang my apron up and scoot off. You going now?

WALTER: No. I'm going to hang around for a bit.

[Louise hangs up her apron, grabs her bags and walks down the shop]

WALTER: I'll unlock the door and let you out.

LOUISE: Okay, Warden. Bye.

WALTER: Ha, ha. Have fun tonight with the hens.

LOUISE: I shall, old man.

WALTER: See you on the news.

An empty sweet shop is an eerie place to be in the evening. The noise of excited customers has melted away and the smell of mint, liquorice and lemon has dissipated. The place is almost haunted – you remember the faces and outlines of customers all around you and yet they've gone. There's a feeling of nothingness. The spirit and heart of the shop has departed.

I'm not keen on hanging around too long because of the shadows. They can play havoc with your senses and you think you can see slight movements among the boxes of truffles. Everywhere is filled with a morose silence except for the odd sound of scratching.

Scratching? I'll kill that bloody mouse!

And Finally

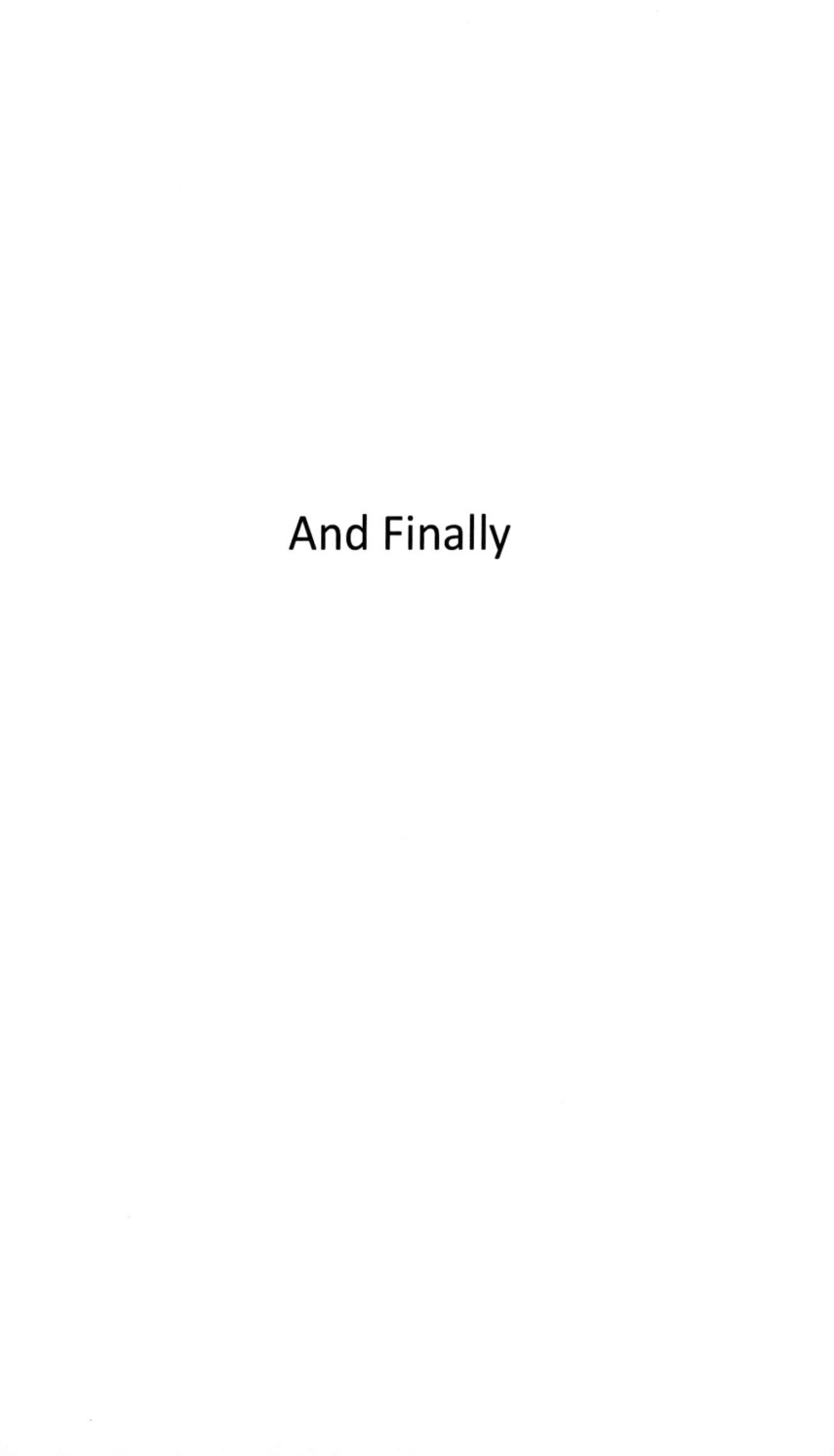

Mary may have had a little lamb but...

Walter had a little van full of chocolate treats;

And everywhere that Walter went,

The kids would buy his sweets.

He drove it to the school one day,

And parked it on the road;

A warden came and booked the van

Despite its special load.

And so poor Walter drove away

But lingered somewhere near;

And waited patiently about

Till children did appear.

"Why do the kids love Walter so?"

The angry warden cries;

Because he flogs them bags of sweets

And bars of Chocolate Fry's.